## Praise for *The Agita*

"Keats wrote, 'Truth is bea[uty]... truth in this book, with characters that can be so painfully honest that at times it seems almost too real. Bronson examines his subject matter unblinkingly, and takes his tale to its tragic conclusion without flinching. Because of that, there is great beauty here, and ultimately this tale shows us what lies at the heart of true courage and heroism."

—David Farland (author of *The Runelords* series)

"*The Agitated Heart* is a sometimes comforting, sometimes heartbreaking story. ... Bronson provides more than lip service to stereotypes and clichés. His characters struggle toward belief—and understanding and acceptance—on every level, constantly stymied by the inadequacy of language even to frame their struggles. ... [B]elief follows pain and fear and effort, and begins the transformation of each character. ... They surpass the limitations of language to approach truth, they move beyond passive statements of belief to actions that are built upon belief."

—Michael R. Collings (emeritus professor, Pepperdine)

"This is Mormon literature in the best sense. A story about a real, terrible family problem and a marriage that is both fraught with problems and eternal. The answers aren't easy and the pain is real, but the storytelling is tender."

—Mette Ivie Harrison (author of *The Bishop's Wife*)

"The best piece of domestic LDS fiction I have ever read. Bronson succeeds in the literary ways: strong and clearly drawn characters, dialogue, and a focused but complex narrative. The narrative POV switches in each chapter between the four main characters, the mother, father, son, and daughter, work well. Often Bronson shows us scenes through two viewpoints, giving the reader greater understanding and charity for the characters. Even without the truly dramatic events of the final chapters, Bronson creates a slice of life of an average Mormon family that fascinated and engaged me. ... It is not often you find literary excellence, emotional heart, and powerful religious messages wrapped up in a single work."

—Andrew Hall (Association for Mormon Letters)

"A moving interconnected tale of love, family, and Christlike sacrifice that examines the nature of love and faith."

—Chris Crowe (author of *Mississippi Trial, 1955*)

"J. Scott Bronson's novella, *The Agitated Heart,* is simply a beautiful, beautiful piece of writing. A troubled but faithful Mormon family struggles to cope with ordinary Mormon challenges; callings in the ward, disputes with ward members, a school bully terrorizing their oldest child. Underlying those tensions is a profound meditation on the atonement, on faith and forgiveness, on hard-heartedness and repentance. Profoundly simple, accessibly rich, human and real and lovely. I know these people. And I ached for them as I read."

—Eric Samuelsen (playright; emeritus professor, BYU)

# The
# Agitated
# Heart

To James—

Dude, I couldn't be happier for all the joy in your life — even if you were my own kid. You do your mama proud.

Merry Christmas from Uncle Scott!

"There is a day of peace."

# The Agitated Heart

J. Scott Bronson

ArcPoint Media
Orem, Utah

ArcPoint Media
Orem, Utah
www.ArcPointMedia.com

Author photo by Paige Afton Bronson
Book and cover design by Marny K. Parkin
Cover image: *Curtain* by Brian Kershisnik, http://kershisnik.com/

Print ISBN: 978-0-9743155-1-5

Printed in the United States of America

*For Renae*
who has finally found her own day of peace

# Contents

## Revelation

We make ourselves a place apart
    Behind light words that tease and flout,
But oh, the agitated heart
    Till someone really find us out.

'Tis pity if the case require
    (Or so we say) that in the end
We speak the literal to inspire
    The understanding of a friend.

But so with all, from babes that play
    At hide-and-seek to God afar,
So all who hide too well away
    Must speak and tell us where they are.

Robert Frost

# Prologue

CHRISTOPHER JACOB ARNOLD SOUGHT PEACE for many days.

## Chapter One

# Sunday Morning

CHRISTOPHER THOUGHT BROTHER PENROD WAS doing a pretty good job of teaching the lesson.

Even if he was old.

In fact, Christopher thought Brother Penrod was probably even better than Brother Archibald, who was the regular teacher for the Valiant 11 class. Brother Archibald never let Chandler Johnson read from the scriptures or anything because Chandler always had a hard time. But on this Sunday, when Chandler tried to get out of reading, Brother Penrod said, "Go ahead, Chandler. You can do it."

So Chandler read.

He stumbled along, as usual, and it wasn't long before Michael Davis lost patience with Chandler's faltering and decided to interrupt. "Where's Brother Archie?" he asked.

Chandler stopped reading and looked up at Michael.

"Michael, that hardly matters at this moment," Brother Penrod said. "You're being very rude."

"Why isn't he here?" Michael apparently didn't care that he was being very rude.

Brother Penrod took a deep breath while he looked at the floor for a minute.

Christopher thought about asking, in silent prayer of course, for some spirit to hold its hand over Michael's mouth.

"Brother Archibald has a sick baby at home so he couldn't come today," Brother Penrod said. "He's sorry that he couldn't make it, I'm sure he'll be glad to know that you miss him, Michael. *I'm* sorry that you're not pleased with your substitute, but I'm about the only man in the ward willing to put up with you in particular, so watch yourself."

Michael snickered.

That made Christopher angry, because he thought Brother Penrod was pretty cool. And besides, today Brother Penrod had brought his colored chalk.

As the lesson had gone along Brother Penrod had created a mural on the board.

Christopher had overheard once that Brother Penrod was a famous artist many years before. None of the other guys in the class thought that was cool the way Christopher did. Except for Chandler, maybe.

Chandler had been reading from the New Testament and now waited to begin again while Brother Penrod added something to the mural.

He was just finishing a large tree on a hillside. He drew fast but with a lot of detail. The tree was old and rough looking. It had several twisted and knotty branches with a few patches of leaves. There wasn't much grass on the hillside, but there was a large bunch of rocks with a squirrel sitting on top of them. And there was a dove in the tree.

Brother Penrod looked up at Chandler and said, "Keep reading."

Chandler looked down at the book and ran his finger around the page trying to find where he'd left off. Christopher leaned over and pointed at the correct verse. "Thirty-nine," he said.

Chandler read haltingly, "'And, he went, a little … a little … further, and fell on his face.'"

Clark Jolley giggled.

Michael said, "What'd he do, trip?"

Everybody in the room laughed out loud at that.

Even Christopher, knowing that Michael's comment was irreverent, smiled a little.

"Hey!" Brother Penrod faced the class with a stern look. "That's enough of that," he said, and held the look until everyone was quiet. "Who are we talking about here?" he asked, pointing at the Bible in Chandler's lap.

"Jesus," Michael said.

"That's right," Brother Penrod said. "And I thought Blazers were more respectful than what I just heard you say."

"What're Blazers?" Michael asked. "We're Valiant 11s." Michael said it with a pretty snotty attitude, and Christopher could tell that Brother Penrod was pretty ticked off.

Christopher thought for sure Brother Penrod was going to come over and kick Michael in the shins. He had done that sort of thing before, and was likely to do it again, even though some parents had complained to Christopher's mom—because she was the Primary president—and to the bishop. But Brother Penrod had been bishop once, a long time before when Christopher was still a baby, and most people in the ward were afraid of him.

But Brother Penrod didn't kick Michael, he mumbled something about Trekkers and Blazers then just looked at Michael until Michael apologized. Brother Penrod looked at Chandler and nodded. Chandler went back to reading and Brother Penrod went back to drawing.

"'. . . he went a little further, and fell on his face, and prayed, saying, O my Father, if it be pos—possible, let this cup pass from me: nev—, never—, never—'"

"Nevertheless," Brother Penrod said without even turning around.

"'Never-the-less, not as I will, but as thou wil—wilt.'"

"All right." Brother Penrod faced the class again.

He had drawn Jesus lying on the ground under the tree, on his stomach, resting on his elbows, with his arms out in front of him, hands together, like a bowl. Jesus's face had a look on it that Christopher had never seen on him before in other pictures.

"What is Jesus about to do?" Brother Penrod asked.

"Get killed," Kraig Dye said.

"Not yet."

Christopher thought he knew the answer but he didn't want to speak up and be wrong. Unconsciously, his fingers touched the Band-aid on his forehead, perhaps feeling for blood.

None of the other boys would make a guess. Just as Brother Penrod was about to tell them the answer Christopher said, "Bleed?"

"What was that, Christopher?"

"Is he going to bleed?"

"Yes, he is. And do you know why?"

Christopher shook his head. The other boys all shrugged.

Brother Penrod pointed at Christopher and said, "What cup does he want to pass from him? What cup doesn't he want to drink from? Why does he look so scared?"

That was it. Jesus looked scared. He looked really, really scared, and suddenly Christopher felt sorry for him. And his fingers went up to his forehead again.

"Do any of you know why Jesus bled from every pore?"

No answers. Not even smart ones.

Brother Penrod's finger moved toward Chandler. "He bled, Chandler, because he suffered for your sins."

And then Brother Penrod took the red chalk and started to add blood to the scene. Blood streaking Jesus's face, dripping from his nose and his beard.

Christopher watched the blood spread and thought, briefly, of the blood that had dripped into his own eyes in a small trickle on Friday afternoon after he had been shoved into the wall at school.

Brother Penrod pointed at Michael, "He suffered for your sins too, Michael."

Blood matted Jesus's hair.

"And your sins, Clark. And yours, Kraig."

Blood soaked Jesus's robes.

"And he suffered for your sins, Christopher, and mine."

Blood filled Jesus's cupped hands and poured down his arms. Christopher hadn't bled very much. Not like this. Christopher only had a scrape, really.

"It's called haematidrosis," Brother Penrod said. "When the soul endures that much stress all the little blood vessels near the surface of the skin break open and blood sweats out of the body. It would have killed you or me. Or anybody."

The dirt around Jesus darkened as the stain spread. Brother Penrod drew a small tear in the dove's eye.

Everyone in the room remained absolutely silent.

Brother Penrod stood back from the chalkboard, looked at it for a second, then walked behind the semicircle of chairs where the boys sat and said, "This is what Jesus did for you, boys. And for me. And for anybody who's ever lived or will live. That's how much he loves us."

Chandler started to sniffle. Clark and Kraig stared at the board. Michael looked down and twisted his fingers.

Christopher looked at the other boys for a moment then turned to the board again. As he gazed at the blood that formed a puddle under Jesus's arms, Christopher felt a pit form in his stomach, yet, at the same time, his heart burned. He looked at Jesus's face, and saw something there besides fear. He thought it might be joy.

Then salty water stung Christopher's eyes and he closed them tight, as if in prayer.

❧

Susan stopped on her way to the nursery and watched as the Valiants lined up in the hall waiting to enter the Primary room for sharing time. She marked how they were rather subdued. In fact, they were very subdued, and Bishop Penrod wasn't even there to keep them in line.

Susan stepped up next to Christopher and said, "Where's Bishop Penrod?"

"He's back in the classroom erasing the chalkboard."

Absentmindedly Susan stroked her son's hair, trying to tame the wild cowlick he had inherited from her. She touched the slightly swollen and reddened skin around the Band-aid, thinking that she was almost glad that Clarence Peterson was inactive. She would love nothing more right now than to tear into that little bully. Christopher held his head still, instead of moving it away from Susan. He was uncharacteristically allowing her to touch him. She lifted his face to look in his eyes. They were a little red. She held her palm to his forehead.

"What's wrong?" she asked.

"Nothing."

Susan glanced at the boy next to Christopher, Chandler Johnson, and noticed that his eyes were red too. In fact, he still had a tear or two welling there.

Susan leaned closer to Christopher and whispered in his ear, "What happened? Did Bishop Penrod kick one of you boys?"

"No, Mom."

"Then why have you been crying?"

Christopher looked over at Chandler, who looked away, then back to Susan, "It was—, it was—, it was 'cause of the lesson."

"What?"

"Never mind, Mom."

Then he put his hands behind his back and leaned against the wall, looking at his feet. Closed off. This was in character.

Fine.

Susan had too much to worry about at the moment to waste time trying to drag an explanation from him now. She had to go settle a problem in the nursery.

Sister Asplund came out of room twelve, the Pandas—no wait—the Butterflies. How would she hold all this stuff in her head? Sister Asplund was a wonderful woman; full of the spirit of service and devotion to her calling, but did she have to revamp the whole nursery? Giving names to the classes, dividing into three classes then back into two, reassigning the teachers, and who knew what else. Susan couldn't keep it all straight.

"Did Gayle find you?" Sister Asplund asked.

"Yes. She said you were having some kind of problem. Is it the Griffiths again?"

"No—, oh, no." Sister Asplund waved her hand. "No, they're just fine now. The changes had them confused for a couple weeks, but they're not complaining any more. It's Geoffrey and Sam."

"What are they doing?" Then suddenly, the din of noise Susan heard coming from room twelve straightened out in her brain and she recognized the sounds and knew the answer to her question before Sister Asplund answered her.

"They're being so wild."

Sister Asplund opened the door to room twelve and Susan nearly laughed at the sight.

Geoffrey and Sam lived next door to each other, and at the age of two and a half had become best friends and enemies. Today they were being friends. Laughing and screeching, they chased each other around the center of the room while the other children and Brother and Sister Griffith stood or sat against the walls watching.

Sister Griffith looked up at Susan and offered a feeble smile.

Susan smiled back and said, "It's like a little tornado in here, isn't it?"

Sister Griffith said, "Yeah," and sighed.

Susan closed the door and said to Sister Asplund, "What do we do, nursery coordinator?"

Sister Asplund threw up her hands. "I don't know. That's why I sent Gayle after you."

This was unusual. In the six short weeks that Sister Asplund had been the nursery coordinator she had taken firm control of things and had not flinched at any of her duties, including taking on the Griffiths. Well, granted, the Griffiths weren't all that intimidating. But what was there about this situation that made her shrink?

"Well," Susan ventured, "why don't we just split them up? Put Sam in the other class."

"That would work except that Todd Daly's in that class and he likes to beat Sam up."

"Move Geoffrey over then."

Sister Asplund made a face. "Joey McGinty's in that class," she said, "and Sister McGinty has asked us not to have Joey and Geoffrey in the same class."

"Oh, that's right." Susan thought for a minute. "Put Joey in Geoffrey's class and Geoffrey in Joey's class."

"Sister McGinty has also asked that we not put Joey in the same class with Lizzy Greahl."

"For heaven's sake, why not?"

"She keeps kissing Joey."

"So?"

"Well, Donna—Sister McGinty—doesn't like it. She thinks it gets Joey, um, uh, excited."

"Oh, please." Susan tilted her head back and stared at the ceiling for a moment, sighing.

"She says—"

"They're not even three years old!" Susan said it so loudly that Brother Higley, teaching Gospel Doctrine in the Relief Society room at the end of the hall, stopped talking and watched Susan for a second.

Susan waved and pantomimed zipping her mouth shut. Then she mouthed the word, "Sorry."

Brother Higley smiled and went back to teaching.

"Sister Asplund," Susan said, "You know that Donna McGinty is..." Susan wanted to say "out of her mind" but caught herself. "You know she's being unreasonable?"

"Well, yes."

"Then we ought to tell her." Meaning, You ought to tell her, Sister Asplund.

Sister Asplund hesitated a moment and said, "I'm her visiting teacher."

Ah. "Say no more."

Rachel Griffith came out of the room and looked at Susan with raised eyebrows.

"Okay," Susan said. "Take Geoffrey out of the Panda room and put him in the Butterflies. Move Joey into the den of iniquity with Lizzy and if he loses his virginity to that little hussy have Donna call me."

Susan turned and headed back to the Primary room but not before catching the expressions on the two ladies' faces. Shock and horror on Rachel Griffith, and a sly little smirk on Sister Asplund.

Susan slipped into her chair at the front of the Primary room and took a deep, contented breath.

The bishop, who sat next to her nervously waiting for his assignment to conduct sharing time, turned to her and asked in a low whisper, "Did you just conquer the foe?"

"Hm? Oh, yeah, I think I did. You may even hear about it later today. I won't be surprised if you do."

The bishop looked bemused and started to say, "What are you talk—" when Cheri Brown, Susan's first counselor—who was conducting—turned to look at them.

The bishop said, "Oops," and sat back in silence.

Cheri's baby, who had been asleep in a car seat under the

little table in the corner, started to fuss. Susan lifted the thin little blanket draped over the car seat handle and hefted the beefy child onto her lap. The bishop offered to hold him and Susan handed him over.

The Junior Primary children were being released to their classes so there was a bit of noise as the piano played and children rustled and whispered in their seats. Yet, over and above all that sound, no one could fail to hear or mistake the horrendous sound—the gaseous and bubbling sound—of Cheri's baby exploding on the bishop's knee.

Horrified, Susan looked down and saw that diarrhea had gone everywhere.

Streaks of it ran down the bishop's leg. A large splotch covered his thigh where the baby had been sitting. The bishop held Cheri's baby up for Cheri to take.

And as Cheri took her child, Susan saw tears in Cheri's eyes.

She's so high-strung, Susan thought. And then had to confess to herself, If that were my child, I would be bawling. Susan had already grabbed Cheri's diaper bag and taken out a few baby wipes. Cheri took the bag from Susan and made a dash for the bathroom.

Susan's second counselor, April Jensen, took Cheri's place in front of the room and continued to shepherd the little children out while trying to shush the older ones who laughed and groaned.

Susan handed a couple wipes to the Bishop and started helping him clean up the mess.

"Well, at least now I won't have to do sharing time," the bishop said.

"Ooh, you're bad," Susan said.

"Kids frighten me. I just don't seem to be able to hold their interest."

"If you stood up there looking like this you'd sure have their interest."

Susan held the soiled baby wipes and looked at the bishop's leg. "There's just too much," she said.

"Yeah, I think I'm going to have to go home and change."

"I think you're right," Susan said. Then she leaned in and muttered so only the bishop could hear, "If this were Marcus, he'd have said the *S* word several times by now."

The bishop smiled and said, "I've always admired your husband's ability to see the real truth in any given situation." The bishop looked down at himself and said, "Now what?"

Susan shrugged. There was no point in trying to clean up any more. She used the last baby wipe to clean her hands.

The bishop said, "Here, I'll take those." He took the wipes from her, looked around the room at everyone and said, "Excuse me," and walked out into the hall.

Sister Jakes had stopped playing the piano and April said something about checking on Cheri, then left. Susan turned to face the Primary and discovered that all eyes were upon her. And all of the twittering stopped. Even Michael Davis shut up when he saw Susan's face. I must look pretty mean, Susan thought. Good.

At the back of the room Susan's secretary, Gayle, stood up and mouthed, "Puppets?"

Susan nodded.

Then she just stared at the kids, unwilling to break the spell of silence. She scanned the children's faces and stopped at Christopher, suddenly remembering the little encounter she'd had with him in the hall earlier.

She had asked why all the Valiant Elevens were so solemn and he'd said that it was because of ... because of the lesson.

Gayle came into the room with the hand puppets—a little boy and a little girl dressed for church—and many of the children cheered.

Susan held up her hand and the cheering stopped. She turned to Gayle and whispered, "Thanks, but I've changed my mind."

What was the lesson about today? Brother Archibald had mentioned it to her when he called to say that Bishop Penrod was taking his class—lesson number thirty.

Susan went to the table in the corner, found her copy of the manual for that class and checked the table of contents. *Jesus Christ in Gethsemane.*

Susan thought furiously for a few seconds, then said, "Okay. Who knows the third Article of Faith?"

Hands shot up. A few kids started to shout, "We believe." Susan shushed them.

Christopher's hand was not up; still, Susan called on him.

"Christopher, why don't you tell us?"

He looked stricken for a moment, but complied, and rattled it off the same way he might some basketball player's vital statistics.

"We-believe-that-through-the-Atonement-of-Christ-all-mankind-may-be-saved-by-obedience-to-the-laws-and-ordinances-of-the-Gospel."

"Very good," Susan said. "And what is the Atonement?"

Christopher was silent for a moment, then he looked at Susan with pain in his eyes, touching his Band-aid, and said, "It's when Jesus bled all over the garden."

❧

Marcus hardly ever needed chalk for his lessons. He had learned long ago that writing lists on the board was generally a waste of time. Nobody ever copied them down, and the rhythm, or the flow, of the lesson was always compromised when he turned his back on the class to write. Marcus liked to face the class and keep the dialogue going.

This Sunday, however, was a chalk day. But there would be no lists. Marcus was going to write one word on the board, one word only—and it was going to be a swear word.

Opening exercises and business—getting people signed up for different assignments and projects—had taken so much time at the beginning of the hour that Marcus had been left with only twenty minutes to give the lesson. He wasn't happy about it but he assured the brethren that he could fit it all in. He'd spent the first five minutes or so setting up the premise, and now he was ready to get into the steak and eggs of the lesson. The swear word.

"Okay, brethren," Marcus said. "Let's make one up. Let's make up our own word that we can use or abuse."

Marcus turned his back on the quorum and stared at the board for a few seconds. But he wasn't worried about ruining the rhythm. He'd built this pause into the lesson, although it wasn't like he planned these things out days in advance. He hadn't thought of the made-up swear word until a quarter of an hour before Priesthood started, while he was preparing the lesson out in the foyer. While everyone else had been in Sunday School.

Marcus began to write S-N-A-F—

"Uh-oh, it's got an F in it," Will Terris said. "I don't know if we should be writing swear words with F's in them, even if they are made up."

Many of the quorum members chuckled.

Marcus turned and looked at his friend and said, "Well, I know a real swear word with an F in it, Will. Shall we use that one instead?"

The entire quorum laughed at that. Brother McGinty didn't laugh but that didn't count.

Will shook his head and waved his hand, refusing Marcus's offer. "That's okay," he said, laughing. "Let's stick with snaf."

"Oh, but I'm not finished," Marcus said. He turned around and completed his made-up word. F-E-N-C-R-A-C-K.

"Snaffencrack?" several of the elders said out loud.

"Yep." Marcus nodded his head a few times while he looked at the word. Then he turned on the quorum and said, "Anything wrong with that you moronic bunch of snaffencracks?"

Some of the men actually looked appalled. Especially Brother McGinty. Marcus reveled in that.

"Which word was more offensive to you?" Marcus asked. "*Snaffencrack* or *moronic*?"

"*Moronic,* of course," Brother McGinty said. "Snaffen-whatever doesn't have any meaning."

"Not yet it doesn't." Marcus looked from Brother McGinty to two or three of the other brethren. Making eye contact with everybody in the class at some point or another kept them relatively interested. "But I can assign it meaning by associating it with certain kinds of words." Marcus turned to Will because Will liked getting picked on and was never offended. "Will, you are one ugly son of a snaffencrack, you know that?"

"So my kids keep telling me."

Chuckles scattered through the room.

Marcus turned to Roberto Hernandez and said, "Will called me last night right in the middle of my favorite show and gossiped for a half-hour about nothing. It was a snaffen waste of my time. Can you believe that?"

"Si," Roberto nodded. "He did the same to me. Called me after he called you."

More chuckles. And even a smile on Joe McGinty's face.

"Brother Joe," Marcus bellowed. "I saw you the other day out in your front yard—you know what I'm talking about—and I've got to say, that was a pretty snaffen stupid thing you did."

Though Marcus was lying through his teeth Brother Joe was abashed.

"What does snaffencrack mean, brethren?"

Carl Whitley raised his hand. "I think it means that other word you were gonna use."

Others agreed and when Marcus swept his eyes across the group he saw that he had everyone's attention. He said, "It probably does, Brother Carl, but the point I'm trying to make is that it doesn't matter. Brother Joe was right. The hurtful words were ugly, waste, and stupid. And yet we have no hard and fast taboos on words like that. Only in the sense that we should not be unkind."

Nods in most quarters.

"You know, I have this book that tells about the origins of things and according to this book some of our taboo words are the result of high-mindedness on the part of the Norman invaders of Saxony back in the eleventh century. The Normans preferred their word, *perspiration,* to the Saxon *sweat.* Even now we say that humans perspire and horses sweat. The Norman word *dine* was better than the Saxons' *eat. Deceased* was better than *dead. Desire* more refined than *want. Urine* more genteel than *piss.*"

Some eyebrows went up.

Marcus smiled. "I can say that one. It's in the Old Testament."

A few of the brethren returned Marcus's smile. Brother McGinty was not among them.

"The Normans considered their word *excrement* far superior to my favorite Saxon word that I won't say here. And of course *fornicate* was nicer than…"

"Snaffencrack," said a new member of the ward whose name Marcus couldn't remember.

"Thank you, Brother." Marcus glanced at Joe McGinty and saw a dark cloud forming there. Perfect. "Who thinks God condemned the Saxons for using such words?" Of course it was a rhetorical question, but Marcus waited for an answer. None came. But it was obvious to Marcus that Joe McGinty wanted to offer one. Or just say something—complain. Marcus looked right at him, with a passive expression; a non-threatening challenge. Brother McGinty did not take it up. "In fact," Marcus continued, "one could reason that those words became R- and PG-rated simply because of Norman pride." Now other members of the quorum were beginning to squirm. Marcus scanned the faces of all the brethren. Two or three of them were smiling. Even nodding. Marcus regretted that he was about to disappoint them. "Now this is not to say that I condone indiscriminate swearing. I don't." At least not publicly I don't, he thought. Not at church. "What I think is important to understand is that any word can be a bad word. It depends on how we use it. We need to be careful with all words. I'll give you an example.

"I devastated Christopher the other day. Absolutely unintentionally. I came home from work and he was there watching *Batman and Robin* and I saw this Band-aid on his forehead and I asked him what happened. He told me how this bully at school had shoved him into a wall and he got this scrape and got blood on his shirt. He thought I was going to be mad or something and he was going to be in trouble. I said, 'You're not in trouble, you goofy little kid.'"

Telling stories on his family, on himself; this was when Marcus really had the attention of the brethren. He was always honest, and nearly always self-effacing. Marcus was not afraid to let them see his faults and use those faults to underscore the main points of his lessons. This let them trust him. Besides, they always stood a chance of hearing something all but scandalous.

Marcus surveyed the attentive faces. "'You goofy little kid.' That doesn't sound so bad does it? I didn't mean it in a bad way, a condemning way. Christopher was practically crying when he said, 'I'm not a little kid.' He didn't care that I called him *goofy*. In our house being goofy is kind of cool. But I meant *little kid* the same way I meant *goofy*."

Marcus paused and gazed, fixed, over the heads of the men, at the window, as if he were watching something outside. But the window was closed, this being the middle of fall, and the glass was textured to mere translucence; there was nothing to see. This pregnant moment was not calculated like some other moments in Marcus's lessons. Marcus remembered very clearly the look on Christopher's face, and a small ache burned Marcus as he stood in front of his brethren.

"You see, gentlemen, as Christopher was growing up, and being a normal little child, doing normal little child things that aggravated the snaff out of me, my constant complaint was 'Christopher, you're acting like a little kid.' I was always angry when I said that. So, in our house, being a little kid is not cool."

Brother Monroe, on the back row, held his watch up—as he did every week per Marcus's request—indicating it was five minutes before the hour.

"Brethren, I submit that we be less concerned about the *spellings* of the words we say and more concerned with the *intentions* of the words we say."

Marcus then challenged the brethren to listen to themselves more carefully in the coming week. He bore a short testimony and called on someone to close the meeting with prayer.

Marcus looked at Brother Monroe as soon as the amens were said. Brother Monroe checked his watch and held up one finger, then a thumbs-up sign. Under by one minute.

Marcus shook hands as the men filed out. He graciously accepted the compliments that came from nearly every one of them. Marcus took particular pleasure in the expression on Joe McGinty's face as he reluctantly offered Marcus a compliment along with everyone else.

"Brother McGinty, thanks for your participation. I hope you're feeling better soon."

"What? I'm fine, I'm—, there's—"

"You looked a little sour there for a second."

Then Marcus dismissed Joe by offering a smile and a handshake to the next brother.

Marcus reveled again. Another rock 'em, sock 'em lesson, with all the right buttons pushed in all the right places. I'm going to go to hell for my pride, Marcus thought. If only Jeff Lakey hadn't told Marcus in PPI that attendance to Elders Quorum had increased dramatically shortly after Marcus had begun teaching the class.

Marcus tried not to revel in that. He kicked himself mentally.

Stay in line you proud son of a snaffencrack.

❧

Kari hated Leah Weisburg.

Well, she didn't hate her, really, she just didn't like the way Leah showed off all the time. Sometimes Sister Merrill didn't even finish asking a question before Leah started doing a butt-dance in her chair, arms waving around like some crazy person.

Kari just wanted to scream at her.

Now here it was almost time for class to be over, and Leah was telling Sister Merrill—the whole CTR-A class—all about how wonderful her baptism was going to be. Leah was the first nonconvert baptism in her family and relatives were coming all the way from New York, even the Jewish ones. Well, they were all Jewish, even Leah, but some of them—like Leah—were only Jewish by birth—by race—not religion, even though before her parents joined the church they were orthodox (whatever that meant), they weren't now, so they weren't Jewish in the spiritual—

*Shut Up!*

Kari didn't scream. Out loud. Just in her head.

Baptism. Baptism. Baptism.

Kari was tired of hearing about baptisms. Really tired. Especially her own. Which was coming up next month.

And Kari didn't want to get baptized. It was just too scary. She couldn't do it. Not yet anyway.

But who was she supposed to tell? How could she tell anybody?

"Kari?"

"Huh?"

"Did you hear me?"

Kari turned from staring at the window to look at Sister Merrill and nodded a little even though she had no idea that Sister Merrill had even been talking.

But Sister Merrill smiled and said, "Kari will be getting baptized at the same time as you Leah. On the same day. And a boy from the Third Ward too. Won't that be fun?"

Kari looked at Leah and Leah frowned with her nose all scrunched up. If she thought no one would see it Kari would have stuck her tongue out at Leah. Instead she just folded her arms in front of her and slumped in her chair, looking away from Leah.

Kari didn't know exactly *why* she was scared to get baptized, she just knew that she was. And she felt like she needed to tell somebody so they could either tell her why she didn't need to be scared, or didn't need to get baptized. But who? Who could she tell? Mom? No way. Daddy? Maybe.

Before she knew what was happening someone had said the closing prayer and everyone was leaving the class. Kari looked out the door from her chair and watched children and adults from two wards—hers going home, and the Third Ward going to Sunday School and Primary—passing by, crowding and talking and laughing and shrieking and hushing. There was just too much going on out there and Kari didn't want to go.

"Kari?"

Sister Merrill stood in front of Kari holding all the pictures and things that she had used for the lesson, her purse, and her scriptures.

Kari looked at Sister Merrill but didn't say anything.

Sister Merrill said, "Will you grab the chalk and eraser and take it to the library for me, please? I can't get it."

Kari nodded.

"Are you all right?"

"Uh-huh."

Sister Merrill entered the hallway and joined the crowd and disappeared.

Kari picked up the little cloth bag containing the chalk and eraser, pulled the drawstring to close it tight, and stood in the doorway, unable to move into the crowd.

Then Christopher appeared at her side and said, "Mom gave me her key. We're supposed to go home together."

"Why?"

"'Cause. Mom has to put all the Primary stuff away. Dad has a PPI, and Mom's gonna walk home with him. Come on."

"I have to take this to the library."

Christopher didn't say anything. He just waited for her to walk down the hall to the library only two doors down, but Kari couldn't move. They stared at each other.

Finally Christopher said, "Come on." And he led her to the library.

Kari walked close to the wall trying not to be seen by anybody. She slipped through the door, dropped the bag in the box on the counter, squeezing past a couple of big fat people from the Third Ward, and got back into the hallway with Christopher.

Christopher already had her jacket. She put it on as they moved down the hall. When she stuck her right arm through the sleeve she bumped into someone and got shoved against the wall. She hit kind of hard but it didn't really hurt because her jacket was so thick. The man who bumped her just kept going, but Christopher stopped and said, "Are you okay?"

She was okay, but she still cried while nodding.

"What's wrong?"

Kari just walked past Christopher and out the door, putting her other arm through its sleeve, and crying as she went down the steps.

"Kari! What's wrong?"

"Nothing!"

Christopher walked beside her without saying anything more. They crossed the street and turned the corner and Kari had not been able to stop crying yet.

Christopher put his arm around her shoulder.

For just a second Kari wanted to jerk away from him, but it *did* feel good to have him so close to her even if he was her brother. Actually he was a pretty nice older brother. He wasn't mean to her very often. And every once in a while he did something really nice. Like this. Kari rested her head against his shoulder for a second. It was nice. But then they had to cross the next street.

"Christopher?"

"Huh?"

"Um, um … what did it—what did it feel like when—when you got baptized?"

"Huh?"

"What did it feel like when, um, when, when you got baptized?"

Christopher looked at her like he didn't understand what language she was speaking. Finally he said, "Wet."

"Tha-tha-tha-that's not what I mean."

"What do you mean, then?"

Kari thought for a second. "I don't know," she said. But then she thought, *But I do know who I can tell that I'm scared.* She looked up at Christopher and he smiled at her. Just not yet, though.

Christopher unlocked the front door of their house and stood back to let Kari in.

Chapter Two

# Sunday Afternoon

CHRISTOPHER WENT TO HIS BEDROOM AND flopped down on the bed without changing his clothes first. He didn't even take his tie off. He lay there, unaware of the physical world—not really seeing the ceiling—thinking about Kari's question.

He knew exactly what Kari meant with her question about baptism, but he didn't know how to give a good answer. He didn't know the *right* answer to her question.

What did it feel like to get baptized?

Wet was the only thing he knew for sure about it. He remembered he had been expecting much more. He had thought there might be choirs of angels, or that the three Nephites might be there or that something—anything—sort of spectacular would occur. But none of that happened.

Wet.

And fast.

Wet and fast was all it had been.

His dad had walked down into the font first, then turned and motioned for Christopher to follow. Christopher walked down the steps into the font watching each foot as it entered the water, wondering if the cleansing process began at this moment or not until the prayer had been said. He looked up into the room hoping to see glowing figures in bright robes but all he saw was a group of little kids, including Kari, crowded up to the font all trying to get the best position for viewing the dunking. Behind the kids were the adults, smiling as if they all held a humorous secret about baptism. Christopher took a deep breath as his father finished the short little prayer. He felt his father's large hands; one wrapped firmly around his wrist, the other spread across his back; one pushing down, the other lifting up. Christopher tried to feel his sins rushing out of his body into the water; tried to picture the water getting dark as though his sins were blood filling the font like the blood in the River Nile in *The Ten Commandments*. But that didn't happen either. As he blinked water from his eyes his dad leaned down and whispered, "Good job, buddy. Let's go." They left the font without applause, without an angel guide, not even a shaft of heavenly light. Maybe the cool stuff happens with the confirmation, he thought.

But, again, he was disappointed.

And yet, lying on his bed, thinking about it three years after the fact, he knew that something had happened. He had felt differently. But, even now, he couldn't think of a way to describe it. He remembered the great weight of all those big hands piled onto his head, and all those big men circled around him. He felt as though something might get crushed; if not his head, surely something with less firmness, perhaps his spirit. But just at the moment when his father said, "Receive the Holy Ghost," Christopher could no longer feel the weight of those heavy hands.

Once, when Christopher had been building a castle out of cardboard and blocks, his dad had come along and said, "Better put another pillar in there or that whole section will fall." Christopher had not yet noticed the sagging platform. His dad knelt with him, pushed up on the sagging section and slipped another block in to support it. He said, "See, you can't just have them out on the sides. You gotta have some in the middle too if you're gonna have it this wide."

But Christopher didn't think Kari would understand if he told her that getting baptized and confirmed was like getting another pillar in your head. In fact, he wasn't sure it made any sense to him either.

Still lying on his bed, Christopher reached up and undid his tie and top button. He slipped his shoes off and kicked them onto the floor.

He wished that his confirmation could have been more like his Aunt Paige's. When they had gone to California in the summer to visit her and all the rest of his dad's family, she had let him read from her journal; her very first journal; her very first entry. He had read it over and over, memorizing it as if it were a verse of scripture. Many of the words had been misspelled and there were too many periods and the penmanship was pretty awful, but the meaning was clear: *To day I got.*

*Bapticed. I felt prod and. Happy. When my. dad gave me the Belesing when he said. I reseved the Holy. gost. I felt him go riright in to me. the end.*

He had asked Aunt Paige, "Did you really feel the Holy Ghost go right into you?"

"Uh-huh. I believe so."

"Wow."

"Did you?"

"I don't know."

Aunt Paige smiled, "I'll bet you did," she said. "You just don't know that you did."

The memory of that felt good. Maybe that's true, he thought, then got up from the bed and changed his clothes.

Christopher wanted very much to feel something; to know that since his baptism, when he had agreed to try to be like Jesus, that the Holy Ghost—or any other good spirit—was involved with his life, was actually helping him somehow to be like Jesus. Because it was so hard to do that. Jesus was the Son of God; he could bleed from every pore and still live. He could feel the guilt of every sin committed by every person who ever lived, now lived, and would live on every one of God's planets and still love all those people.

Christopher lay back on the bed again and thought about the very end of Brother Penrod's lesson. They had read in the book of Luke about Christ in the garden; about how he had asked God to take away the cup of sins because he was so frightened. But then an angel came and gave him strength, and then, Brother Penrod said, "The cup was poured out upon him."

Right out loud, still staring at the ceiling but not seeing it, Christopher said, "I wish an angel would come to me."

❧

Susan liked it when Marcus held her hand. It was a simple gesture, a light touch, but with their fingers interlocked, it was an intimate gesture and touch unfettered by urges and desires. It tingled the hairs on the nape of her neck and warmed her whole body. And it made her feel as though she belonged to Marcus, and she liked that feeling a lot. Certainly not politically correct, she thought, but right and good nonetheless. The scriptures said that she owned him and he owned her, and while after twelve years of marriage they were still trying to figure out exactly what that meant, it was a comforting thought. So she held on to it as tightly as she held Marcus's hand as they walked through the brisk autumn air toward home, the long way. The wind whipped her hair into her face. Rather than reach up and pull it back with her hand she leaned against Marcus and used his shoulder to sweep the hair from her eyes.

"Did you just wipe your nose on me?" he asked.

Susan giggled. "Uh-huh."

"Okay."

And they walked on a few more steps without comment, then Susan really did wipe her nose on Marcus's shoulder.

He stopped and glanced down at her and she froze in midwipe. "You are really disgusting," he said in his calm, nonchalant voice. "I'm going to have to spank you when we get home."

"Promises, promises." She leaned back, holding his hand even tighter, and rubbed his shoulder with her other hand. "Nothing there," she said. "Gotcha."

Marcus leaned down to kiss her but instead licked one of the lenses of her glasses.

"Ahgg!"

"Looks like I got you," he said smugly.

Susan took her glasses off and wiped the slobbery lens on Marcus's shoulder then gave him a firm swat on the behind.

"Ooh, thank you. And in public even."

Susan laughed. "You're demented," she said, taking his hand again.

"Isn't that why you married me?"

"Uh-huh."

As they completed their walk around the block, Susan relished the muted Sunday sounds that whispered to her from cross streets, distant back yards, and tall deciduous trees. Jazz music came from the open window of the Wanamakers' living room. Someone was burning cedar in a fireplace somewhere, but Susan detected no other scents in the chilly air. In the gray sky clouds moved aside to let the sun make a perfunctory effort to warm the earth. As they came upon their own house, Susan noted the naked lawn and regretted that they didn't get the wooden lawn furniture they had considered buying. It would have been nice to sit outside for a while under the birch, reading scriptures, chatting with passing neighbors out for a Sunday stroll, even on a zephyrous day such as this.

"Is *zephyrous* a word?"

Marcus stopped in his tracks. "What?"

"Zephyrous."

He shrugged, shaking his head; his what-in-the-world-are-you-talking-about gesture.

"You know, from the Winnie-the-Pooh video."

"I am completely lost, Susan. I have no idea what you're talking about."

Susan sighed. This was one of those "little" things about Marcus that irritated her at times. There were no toothpaste tube problems in their house, just awareness problems. In all fairness, Marcus had the same complaint about her. Each of them thought the other should be more aware of the kinds of things that interested them.

"In the *Blustery Day* video," she explained, "Owl mentions a zephyr."

"What's a zephyr?"

Susan uttered a mock gasp. "You don't know what a zephyr is? You're the smart one in this family; you're the college graduate; I should think you would know this."

"Ha, ha, ha. What's a zephyr?"

"A wind," she answered a bit too proudly. "A gentle wind."

"Okay. And what's your question again?"

"Is *zephyrous* a word?"

Marcus lifted his chin to show that he was putting his college-educated brain to work. He glanced quickly at her with his thinking frown firmly in place.

Susan nearly giggled. This little game was so old and comfortable that for a fraction of a second she saw themselves back in their first apartment, sitting on the couch, Marcus expounding on some profound thought he'd just concocted.

Susan couldn't be sure if the goose bumps that stood out on her arms now were a reaction to the warmth and thrill of that memory or to the slightly chilling caress of the currently swirling fall zephyr.

"Zephyrous, huh? Meaning," he said, "that the wind has a zephyr-like quality?"

Susan nodded.

"Zephyritic—"

"Sounds like a disease."

"Zephyrite."

"From the Book of Mormon?" Susan asked.

"Yes. That group that was all talk and no substance? You know, full of hot air?"

"Oh, boo."

"Zephyrous. Hey, if it communicates, it's a word. That's what words are for."

Suddenly the game was over. Marcus had just found a Truth to declare. It wasn't a Grand Truth by any means—that would have taken at least ten minutes—but a Simple Truth, one that should be obvious to any thinking, reasoning being by Marcus's judgement. And with just a moment's thought Susan found that she agreed with him. And her admiration for him rebloomed within her. Not that her admiration for Marcus had died or even dwindled over the years, but it did close up from time to time and she needed simple moments like this to remind her that he truly was *not* like most men. Which had been her first serious attraction to him. She hoped that Christopher was paying attention. Marcus truly was a good example of what a husband and father should be.

Even though the air wasn't that cold, a pleasant shiver shot up Susan's spine and her goose bumps got goose bumps. She hugged Marcus's arm to her and said, "Let's go inside."

∼

Marcus couldn't wait to get into the house. Not because of any phobias or hatreds he felt toward anything to do with the out -of-doors; that wasn't it at all. Marcus loved nature; he loved being outside, in the thick of the Earth, though he would never classify himself as an outdoors man. In fact he had quite enjoyed the little walk around the block with Susan; the contact, the conversation, the cool grayness of the day, the gentle zephyrous winds—though, by Susan's definition, calling a zephyr gentle would be redundant—and the utter lack of anxiety through it all. It had been an easy stretch of walking and talking. No, Marcus was eager for the interior because he was a caveman and he liked his cave. Especially on Sunday afternoons.

They got inside and Susan went to check on the kids even though they really didn't need to be checked on. That was one of the things about Sunday afternoons that Marcus liked. The kids were old enough now that they didn't require the same amount of attention that they had in the early years. They were trained now to pursue worthy activities for a Sunday afternoon; pursuits such as his own.

They could read pretty much anything they wanted; Marcus and Susan didn't have much of anything that could be considered terribly damaging to the soul. Granted there was adult literature in the house, and plenty of it, but not adult in the same sense that society had adopted. Michener, Clavell, Tyler, Smiley, Irving all took up space on the shelves and someday the kids would be old enough to be able to read those books if they so desired. But for the time being Lewis, Wilder, L'Engle, Burnett, Burroughs, and others were satisfying the literary tastes of the kids.

Certain videos and TV shows were allowed on Sundays. Letter or journal writing, drawing, puzzles, board games, some outdoor activities (no bikes or skates); all approved by Marcus and Susan for the Sabbath.

Eating and sleeping were Marcus's personal favorites. His ideal Sunday followed this course usually: cereal, church, a light lunch, watching *Sunday Morning*—which he had recorded, a couple hours of sleep, some reading, dinner, family television viewing, husband and wife television viewing, then more sleep. It doesn't get any better than this, he thought. He was truly grateful that the Sabbath was made for man, not man for the Sabbath.

As Marcus shed the stiff Sunday-go-to-meeting entrapments for his exquisitely comfortable junk clothes, Susan came into the room.

"Kari's reading her scriptures and Christopher's asleep."

Marcus smiled inside and thought, the kid learns fast. He's gonna be all right.

ᴂ

Kari loved the scriptures.

She didn't love reading them, but she really liked some of the stories in them when Mommy or Daddy or Sister Asay or Grandpa or Grandma Snyder or anybody would tell them without all the scripturey talk. Grandpa and Grandma Arnold had given Kari and Christopher a set of books that were sort of kids' versions of the Book of Mormon. They were all right, but they were still kind of hard to read and sometimes the pictures were boring. And they couldn't help her today.

Today she needed answers and, even though they were hard to understand, Kari had borrowed Daddy's big thick heavy book that had all the scriptures in it. She had taken it to her room and set it on the little desk that Daddy had brought home from a yard sale or DI or someplace. And then she sat and looked at it, afraid to open it. At other times, when Kari had had questions about things to do with Church or the stories from the scriptures, Mommy or Daddy would sometimes look things up in the scriptures to find the answers. Kari knew there was a section that listed scriptures according to what they were about, but she didn't know what it was called or where exactly it was in this big book. She knew where the maps were so she went there first.

After the maps was the Book of Mormon. Before the maps was the Bible Dictionary. She went back to the maps and flipped through them without looking at them, trying to think. She turned pages through the Book of Mormon, being real careful because the paper was so thin. After the Book of Mormon was the Doctrine and Covenants and then the Pearl of Great Price, and then the Index. Maybe this was it.

Kari began turning the pages again, one at a time, looking for words that started with the letter B. On page fourteen she was still in the A section and a word caught her eye: anger. She remembered the last time Mommy had set her and Christopher down and taught them from the scriptures. They had been fighting and Kari had said something about wishing that a giant bird would come and take Christopher away and eat him. Mommy had looked so sad when she had brought Kari and Christopher into the living room to sit together on the couch. After a minute she had stood and said, "You kids wait here for a minute, I'll be right back. And don't touch each other. Don't even look at each other."

Easy, Kari thought, and she twisted her neck and lifted her chin so that she was looking as far from Christopher as she could.

Mommy came back into the room, sat down and opened her scriptures. "Let's see," she said. "Let's see what the Book of Mormon says about anger. Ah, here it is." Then she turned a bunch of pages until she found what she was looking for. She read to herself for a minute, then she looked up at Kari and Christopher. This was when she looked so sad.

Mommy said, "It says here that my children are of the devil."

A terrible thrill shot through Kari's stomach. Her head felt really hot, like it was going to melt. She looked at Christopher. He looked like he was going to cry and suddenly Kari felt the same way.

"Listen to this," Mommy said. "'He that hath the spirit of contention'—Do you know what contention is?"

Kari shook her head.

"To contend is to fight. Someone with the spirit of contention is someone who is angry a lot and wants to fight all the time. 'He that hath the spirit of contention is not of me'—not of God—'but is of the devil, who is the father of contention, and he stirreth up the hearts of men to contend with anger, one with another.'"

Kari began to feel an ache in her stomach—not like she was going to throw up or anything—but a feeling like a great sadness or something. Maybe a feeling like what Kari saw in Mommy's eyes.

Since that day Kari had tried so hard to not be angry any more, or at least not to contend with anyone when she was angry. Mommy had said that if she was angry she could pray and tell Heavenly Father how angry she was. He would listen. Mommy said, "We girls like to tell people how we feel but nobody likes to listen as much as Heavenly Father does. I'll listen to you too, but sometimes I forget that I should. Heavenly Father never forgets, okay?"

Now Kari felt that same sadness in her stomach, but it wasn't anger that caused it this time. She was afraid.

Maybe I should look up *afraid* instead of *baptism,* she thought. She turned back a few pages and found *afraid. See also fear,* it said. There weren't very many things about *afraid* and it took her a while to figure out that the *a.* referred to the word *afraid.* Then the little parts of sentences made more sense. She looked up *fear* and scanned through the sentences. "Fear not the reproach of men. Many durst not steal for fear of law. Awful fear of death fills breasts of the wicked. Fear not what man can do. Perfect love casteth out fear."

Kari's heart stopped.

Perfect love casteth out fear.

I can never do that, she thought. I can never have perfect love.

Again, she remembered back to the scripture about anger. Mommy had said, "Will you kids try not to be contentious? Try not to be angry so much? Please?"

They had both nodded and said, "Yes."

But Kari still felt anger all the time while Christopher hardly ever got angry any more. He probably never felt fear either. Somehow he had found perfect love. I wish I could be like him, she thought.

Chapter Three

# Sunday Evening

CHRISTOPHER SAW THE ROBIN THROUGH THE living room window.

It sat in the shadow of the tree in the front yard. It wobbled in place, looking as if it couldn't keep its balance. Its mouth opened every time it breathed, and it breathed rapidly. Even though he was in his pajamas already, and barefoot, Christopher went outside to get a closer look.

The bird barely noticed Christopher's approach. Its eyes remained shut except for half a moment when Christopher stroked its wing. It started a bit at his touch but made no effort to escape from him. Christopher squatted there in the grass with his arms folded over his knees and watched the bird for a couple of minutes.

He heard the screen door open then slam shut but he didn't turn to see who it was.

"Um, um, um, what's wrong—what's wrong with it?"

Kari squatted next to Christopher.

"I don't know," he said. "I think it's dying."

"Why?"

"I don't know."

"Did-did somebody shoo-shoot it?"

"I don't think so. I don't see any blood."

"What are you kids doing out here?" Mom called to them as she came out of the house. "You're in pajamas, you don't have any shoes or sweaters on, and it's cold and nearly dark. What are you think—, oh, my."

Mom squatted with Christopher and Kari and after a few seconds said, "The poor thing."

"What should we do with it, Mom?" Christopher asked.

"I don't know. What's wrong with it?"

"It's, it's dying," Kari said.

"Are you sure?" Mom asked.

"Christopher said so."

Mom reached out like she was going to touch the bird but pulled her hand back and just watched it with a sad expression on her face. "Christopher may be right," she said.

Christopher looked over at his mom and asked, "Do you think we can save it?"

"How?"

"Digging up some worms for it, or something."

She shrugged. "I don't know. That's a good idea, though. Go ahead." Then, just before she stood and turned toward the house to go back in, Christopher thought he saw a tear in her eye. Why would his mom cry about a sick bird?

Susan stepped into the house and wiped a tear from her cheek.

Why am I crying about a sick bird? she thought.

From outside Susan heard Christopher say, "Don't touch it, don't touch it. Let's just go get it some worms."

Susan wiped her eyes and stuck her head out the door and called to the kids as they headed around the side of the house toward the shed, "Hey! Get some shoes and sweaters on at least. Okay?"

"Okay," they yelled together. Then Susan heard them come in the house through the back door and nearly collided with them as they dashed down the hall to their rooms. While they got their shoes and sweaters Susan went out to the shed and found the little garden shovels for them. Just as she came out of the shed the kids burst through the back door, practically tripping on each other.

"Here you go," Susan said, holding out the shovels. "I'll go in and turn on the back light for you." Then she pointed and said, "Dig on that side of the garden, all right?"

"Okay," Christopher said, looking a bit confused. "Thanks, Mom."

"You're welcome," Susan said, and almost added, Don't look so shocked, I can be nice sometimes.

And away they went, embarking on a solemn and thrilling adventure.

Susan watched them for a few moments thinking, Though I should be nice more often than I am usually. Then she went into the house, turned on the flood lights that illuminated the entire back yard, and returned to the living room. She was fine until her eyes adjusted to the contrast between the buttery interior light and the cool pastels of twilight outside, and she saw the robin teetering in the shadows on her lawn. Then a small involuntary sob erupted from her and she turned from the windows and sat on the couch.

For a couple of minutes, the robin had been merely an abstract concern, something that existed only in thought, in concept, in her children's adventure. It became real again when she saw it gasping for life. And Susan cried, not because she knew the robin would die, but because she knew that Chritopher and Kari could not save it. She cried for the futility of their selfless efforts.

No matter what they did, no matter how hard they tried, that bird was going to die.

❧

Marcus had chosen, as the subject of his dissertation, dysfunctionalism. The premise of his thesis was that everybody was dysfunctional; every family was dysfunctional in some form or another. When modern psychobabble was applied to human behavior, the inevitable conclusion was that everyone was sick. And while he was sure that some of his colleagues would disagree, Marcus thought his own family was more stable than some might think. Most of the time.

From his office—slash—corner-of-the-semi-converted-garage, Marcus heard Susan crying in the living room. He debated with himself as to the proper course of action. Should he charge out there to demand how the children had offended or slighted her, or should he quietly enter the room and sympathetically inquire about her latest personal crisis?

Well, maybe that wasn't fair.

While it was true that Susan cried a lot, it was also true that she never cried in order to manipulate a person or situation. Susan was a sensitive person who felt deeply about many things. Marcus recalled how she had cried, off and on, for a week after their good friend, Bill, had up and moved to Seattle with only a couple days' warning. With Bill gone Marcus had lost the only friend, at the time, who truly understood Marcus. The kids had lost a surrogate uncle, and Susan had lost her oldest child. Together Susan and Marcus had decided that Susan's maternal inclination toward Bill had been betrayed by his sudden and complete departure. Marcus knew that there were many husbands who would have felt jealousy or even rage if their wives had reacted the way Susan had. But Marcus thought it was sweet. He loved her for it.

And when it came to crying, well, the simple fact was that some people were criers and others were not. The Arnold family was a family of criers: Susan, definitely; Kari, of course; Christopher, a little; and Marcus—being honest with himself—well, he was pretty good at it too. Susan had often claimed (once, in a Sacrament meeting talk) that she had finally agreed to marry Marcus only because he had cried through most of the *Anne of Green Gables* miniseries.

Marcus refocused on his computer screen and counted the lines he had added to his dissertation in the last hour.

Wow.

Six whole lines.

He saved them before stepping into the hall that lead to the living room. He stood at the door of his office for a second, listening to the computer whir and hiss and click, and told himself to remember to be calm and not get worked up, or over-wrought, no matter how emotional this encounter might become. He was never able to be of any help to Susan if he was competing with her emotionally. Nothing ever came of the game of "I'm more hurt by you than you are by me." Still, it was too easy to fall into that trap. It took vigilant mental effort to keep from doing so.

He found Susan sitting on the couch, wiping tears from her face with the corner of one of the throw pillows.

"What's wrong, Sweetie?" he asked.

"Oh, nothing. I'm being stupid."

"What about?"

"That—," she waved an arm toward the windows, "—that silly bird."

Marcus glanced out the window, but without anything more specific than an arm wave, he had no idea where to look. "What bird? Where?" he said.

"Next to the tree trunk. On the grass."

Then Marcus saw it; a shivering little robin. "What happened?"

"I don't know. It's just dying."

"Are you sure?"

Susan shrugged, and fresh tears spilled down her cheeks. She wiped them away and laughed derisively.

Marcus went outside and examined the bird. The examination consisted of nothing more than squatting next to the bird and looking at it for a couple of minutes, touching it once. There were no signs of blood so it hadn't been shot. When Marcus touched it, it turned its head, so it hadn't broken its neck. It simply sat, not even trying to escape, opening its mouth to suck in each little spasm of breath. Susan was right; it was dying. But it didn't seem like a Susan thing to cry over a dying bird.

When he got back inside, Marcus asked, "Are you sure it's just the bird you're crying about?"

Susan didn't say anything for a minute, but she cried a little harder. Finally she said, "No, I'm crying because I'm a mean and selfish person."

Oh, brother. "Why do you say that?"

"Because that's what everyone believes."

"Everyone, who?"

"Everyone, everyone."

Marcus didn't say anything for a minute. Then he said, "And this dying bird has brought you to this realization?"

Susan nodded.

"How?"

Susan looked down and picked at her fingernails while she got her crying under control.

Marcus did not interrupt her process. He knew that she wanted to talk about this; she just had to do it in her own time. He watched her chew a sliver off one of her nails and spit it onto the floor. He waited patiently for two or three minutes.

During those silent minutes, Christopher and Kari came into the front yard with a few worms and tried to feed them to the robin.

Susan turned and watched the kids for a few seconds. "It's not going to work," she said. "It won't eat the worms, and it'll die." Then she turned to face Marcus again; well, face the room. She looked at her hands when she spoke. "You think I'm mean and selfish because I want everybody to live a certain way."

Marcus tried not to show any emotion, but she was right. Somewhat. There were times when he thought that she was mean and selfish, but he had never told her that. He suspected though that, more than her being able to know his thoughts, it was easier for her to say "you think I'm selfish," than it was to say, "I am selfish."

"Maybe I am," Susan said. "Maybe I am mean and selfish."

Still, Marcus didn't speak or show any emotion. He just did his best to look attentive. Which wasn't very difficult since he was very interested to see how this thought would play out. For the moment Susan was showing remarkable control. And remarkable insight, he thought.

Susan looked up at Marcus and said, "No, I *am* mean and selfish. Sometimes."

Marcus looked down, just in case a look of triumph or something like it revealed itself to Susan.

"I think, though," she said, "It's just because…" She remained silent for some time, still picking at her finger nails. "I don't want to lose anybody."

Okay, Marcus thought, I think I'm following this, but where does the bird come in?

"I want to keep everybody together. I don't want anybody to get lost along the way. But I can't do that any more than they'll be able to save that bird."

"Along the way to where?" Marcus asked. He had decided it was now safe to interject without inadvertently inhibiting Susan's discourse.

"Heaven. The Celestial Kingdom. Paradise."

Ah.

"I want us all to be there together, Marcus."

Then Marcus spoke without thinking. "And none of us will make it without you to lead us there."

Susan finally looked into Marcus's eyes, and the pain he saw there was bitter, and deeply felt.

Marcus wanted to apologize. He wanted to crumble beneath the weight of her wounded gaze. He wanted to turn back time. But he couldn't do any of those things. He couldn't speak. He couldn't even look away.

"Actually, Marcus, I was thinking that *I'll* never make it there without *you* to lead me." Then Susan stood up and left the room leaving a cold, dark void to form in the pit of Marcus's stomach.

Marcus swore and raged at himself in his heart and in his mind.

❧

Kari hated worms.

Well, she didn't hate them, she just didn't like the way they wiggled around in her hand. So now they sat in a squirmy little pile in front of the robin while Christopher tried to get the robin to eat one.

Christopher dangled the worm in front of the robin's beak saying, "Come on little robin. Take a bite. Take a bite."

But the robin only opened its mouth to breathe and kept its eyes closed except when the worm tapped it on the head.

Kari heard the front door open. She turned and watched Daddy come out of the house and across the lawn to stand beside her and look at the bird.

"It's sick, Daddy," she said.

Daddy put his hand on Kari's head and said, "I think you're right, sweets. And I don't think it's going to get better."

"What do we do, Dad?" Christopher asked.

"What do *you* think?" Daddy said.

Christopher shrugged. "I don't know."

Daddy squatted down, rubbed his chin and pulled on his beard. "Well," he said, "it's not going to live. It'll just sit here in pain until it dies, or until a cat finds if and eats it."

Kari gasped. She pictured in her head what it would look like if the Fulcinetti's big, fat, yellow cat came and ripped the bird's head off and started eating it.

She used to like that cat.

Daddy put his hand on Kari's head again and said, "Don't worry, sweets, I won't let any cats get it."

"Okay."

And they all sat there real quiet for a minute. Then Christopher said, "What are you going to do, Dad?"

"Well, I think the best thing to do, because it's feeling so much pain, is to just put it out of its misery—"

"What—what, what is that?" Kari asked.

"He's gonna kill it," Christopher said.

"Daddy?"

He looked kind of upset for a second and said, "Sweetheart, it really is the kindest thing to do."

"Why?"

"He won't feel it. I promise. And right now he's really hurting. I can make that hurt stop."

Kari looked at Christopher, and he looked at her.

Daddy said, "Why don't you kids go in the house. I'll take care of the bird."

Kari and Christopher kept looking at each other. Finally Christopher looked down and got up and went into the house.

Kari watched him go then looked at Daddy. She wanted to say something, ask something, tell him something, but she didn't know what. She wanted to know why the bird was sick, why they couldn't save it and why Daddy had to kill it. She wanted to try to think of something else to do to it, or wish that it was on someone else's lawn so they would have to kill it instead. She wanted to tell Daddy that she still loved him even though he was going to kill the robin. Kari didn't say any of those things though. She just went into the house, into her room.

After sitting on the bed for a few minutes, feeling really sad, she heard Daddy getting into the shed. She went to the window and after a minute saw Daddy come around the side of the house toward the garden. He had his garden gloves on and carried the big shovel in one hand and the robin in the other. He set the robin down on the ground, laying it on its side. Its breathing was even faster now. Daddy dug out a hole in a bare part of the garden and stood there for a minute looking at the robin. For a second Kari thought that he would change his mind and not kill the bird, but all of a sudden he lifted up the shovel and brought the point of it down real hard and real fast on the robin's neck. Kari's body jerked, almost as if the shovel had hit her instead of the robin. The bird's head flew into the hole Daddy had dug, and the legs kicked a couple of times before Daddy pushed the body into the hole with the shovel. Then he covered it up.

Kari pulled the curtains closed when Daddy turned to come back to the house. She peeked through a little slit and saw him wipe his eyes on his sleeve as he passed by her window.

With tears on her cheeks Kari fell back on her bed, holding her throat with one hand, trying to rub away the pain that grabbed her there.

## Chapter Four

# Monday Morning

CHRISTOPHER FOUGHT THE URGE TO MOAN AND complain. And he succeeded. He didn't say a thing as his mother placed the plate in front of him. Not a single negative peep.

His face, on the other hand, he knew was not able to hide his feelings. In fact his whole body gave him away. He took one look at the plate and his shoulders sagged, his legs fidgeted, his lip curled, and his eyes shut as if he were in pain. But no sound came out. When he opened his eyes his mom was watching him. He sat up straight, but he couldn't change the pained expression.

"I don't care if you don't like potatoes, Christopher, you *will* eat some of those hash browns."

Christopher knew better than to protest. He just stared at the steaming little pile of crusty potatoes. In preparation for a big sigh, he took a deep breath and the smell almost made him gag.

"Here," Dad said, opening the bottle of ketchup, "squirt some of this on it. Then it won't taste so bad."

Yes it will, Christopher thought. Nothing can make potatoes taste good.

"I don't understand it," Mom said, as she moved around the kitchen, setting things on the table, moving things from the counter to the sink, to the trash; basically, just never standing still. "You like french fries and potato chips."

Well, that was true.

"*I* like hash browns," Kari said, sliding into her chair.

Christopher glared at Kari and she shoved her smile at him.

Dad said, "Well, bully for you, Kari."

"Yes, Kari," Mom said, "we know how much you like hash browns."

Kari shut up and sulked for a second—only a second. Then she said, "Can-can, can I say, say the blessing?"

"Sure," Dad said, "but wait 'til we're all ready."

And then there was silence around the table while they all sat in their chairs waiting for Mom to sit down.

Christopher just stared at his bleeding hash browns. Out of the corner of his eye he saw Kari moving around. He looked up and watched her fidget with her plate and silverware. She kept moving everything—rearranging. Never very much, just slight differences in angle or distance. And she was making a great show about being very particular, her head tilted to one side and then the other as if she were checking various views, her other fingers extended while the forefinger and thumb daintily placed the fork just here; no, there, then her hand floating high in a sort of salute to etiquette. A few more seconds of having to watch that and Christopher was sure he would explode. He wanted to shout, "Quit your fussing!" the way Dad usually did.

Christopher glanced at his dad. Dad's eyes were closed. No wonder he wasn't going nuts.

In his head, Christopher *did* shout, Mom, hurry up and sit down so we can eat! For as much as he hated potatoes, Christopher loved french toast and sausage and his stomach was growling for food.

❧

Susan knew that they were all anxious to eat. While she moved around in the kitchen she sensed that they were waiting furiously for her to sit down so they could dig in; especially Christopher. The way his legs alternated between swinging madly, then wrapping around the legs of the chair, and the way he breathed like a little bulldog, and the way he stared at his sister's fidgeting as if he could blow her to smithereens just by looking at her, all but shouted at Susan to sit down.

But this was Monday Morning Breakfast. Marcus didn't have to teach his first class until ten o'clock, and the kids' school started at nine-thirty, so at eight-thirty every Monday Susan fixed a big breakfast so they could all sit down and eat together.

Family Home Morning.

And Susan would not sit down until everything was just right.

No spreads in jars. Jellies, preserves, and butters all had been dished into small serving bowls. Even the syrup had been heated and poured into the ceramic elephant—a family heirloom Susan had received from her grandparents as a wedding present. As a child Susan had loved pouring syrup onto her pancakes from that little elephant's trunk. Now her kids were just as tickled by the thing. Even Marcus got a kick out of pouring "elephant snot" on his waffles and pancakes and whatever. The kids giggled and gagged every time Marcus asked for it that way, and Susan always said, "Marcus. Please." But she smiled, because there was that moment just after he said, "Somebody pass me the elephant snot," when every member of the family was smiling, enjoying themselves, forgetting about everything except the hilariously disgusting thought of Dad eating elephant snot. It was a macabre moment when the family was united as a strange little community of snot eaters.

And Susan had to have the counters cleared before she would sit down. Not everything washed and put away necessarily; just out of sight, in the sink or refrigerator, or somewhere.

Christopher's eyes were pinched shut in a painful grimace while his legs swung frantically under his chair. Susan slipped into her chair quickly and quietly before he opened his eyes. She smiled to herself when she saw the look on his face when Kari began her blessing on the food. Susan felt an inkling of guilt about having her eyes open as the prayer started, and a couple inklings about enjoying Christopher's consternation at missing the beginning of the prayer.

She and Marcus had discussed this competitive nature of hers a few times, and while, intellectually, she knew it was wrong to act out against her own children, emotionally she was still an insecure ten-year-old living with her grandparents and a jealous, vindictive, fourteen-year-old aunt. Sometimes Susan wished that Marcus would let her blame her parents for dying and leaving her in that awful situation. Most of the time, though, she knew he was right.

Kari's prayer was finished in about three and a half seconds. And for three and a half minutes after that hardly a word was spoken around the table—only requests for margarine, apple butter, jelly, elephant snot, and so forth—as everyone prepared their french toast and started eating.

Marcus took a long drink from his juice and said, "By-the-way," and Susan knew instantly, without Marcus having to say her name, that he was talking to her. This was one of the many phrases, and one of the many tones that he used to talk to *her*. For half a second Susan was struck by how amazing it was for them to have developed such subtle and effective short-cuts of communication. "The bishop called you yesterday, while you were at choir practice."

"Yeah," Susan said around a mouthful of potatoes. "I talked to him later, while you were home teaching."

"What did he want?" Marcus asked.

"Just to tell me that Donna McGinty called him to complain about me." Susan said it nonchalantly, to indicate to Marcus that she wasn't taking it too seriously, because for some stupid reason he seemed to take it personally when she got upset by what other people thought of her (especially the McGintys), even though she was actually riled and a little depressed about it.

"What did you do this time?"

"Oh, I let Joey in the same room with that little slut Lizzy Graehl."

Marcus's eyebrows went up and he glanced at the children then back to Susan. She knew this was his way to chastise her without actually having to say anything negative in front of the children. Later, probably as they were getting into bed, he would say something like, "You know, you shouldn't speak so candidly in front of the children. They remember that kind of stuff." And he would be right of course, and that would make her angry. She wouldn't be angry that he would be right; she would be angry that she didn't stop to think about the fact that she hadn't considered the ears in the room before speaking. She didn't want to have to think about that kind of thing. Often times Susan felt that it would be oh so nice if she could go through life acting on her feelings without having to consider others' feelings in the process. Why couldn't people just deal with her feelings as they came? My feelings are who I am, she thought. Why can't people just accept me for who, or what I am? Children and husbands included. That's why she would be angry. And it would ease the guilt that always accompanied her self-directed anger if she directed it at Marcus instead, for so coyly reminding her that she was a rotten, selfish human being.

"I see," Marcus said, sliding a piece of sausage around his plate, through the elephant snot, then lifting it, dripping, to his mouth. A drop of syrup fell onto his beard and seeped through the whiskers as he said, "And how did Lizzy acquire such a reputation?"

"It's all in Donna's mind," Susan said. "She's wacko."

Susan didn't even want to see the look Marcus gave her for that. She hacked a portion from her french toast and stuffed it into her mouth. *Then* she glanced up to see Marcus staring at her. There was absolutely nothing to read in his expression and that was more maddening than a judgmental sneer. Susan returned his gaze, blank for blank and blink for blink.

Marcus glanced at Christopher, so Susan glanced at Christopher. He had finished his french toast and sausage and was now piddling around with his hash browns. Just eat them! she screamed in her head.

"Christopher," Susan said, "tell us about Bishop Penrod's lesson yesterday."

❧

Marcus stopped chewing and stared at Susan, this time not even trying to hide his feelings.

When Susan shot a look back at him, Marcus narrowed his eyes, trying to give her the message that he didn't like being ignored this way. But she ignored him and turned back to Christopher.

Christopher looked like he'd just been caught doing something wrong. Marcus felt pity for the child, though not enough to let him not eat his potatoes. Potatoes were cheap and good for the body. The kid would just have to learn to like them. But to have to eat a food that makes you gag and get grilled by your mother at the same time was almost too much.

Christopher didn't speak. And his expression pled with Marcus to save him from a fate worse than death. But Marcus couldn't very well start contradicting Susan right now or the tension that had begun to brew the previous evening would become a boiling pot of cold shoulders and hard stares. I started this last night, he thought, I ought to try to finish it.

"So," Marcus said, "Bishop Penrod taught your class yesterday, huh?"

"Uh-huh."

"Did he kick anybody?"

"No."

"That's too bad. Michael Davis could use some kicking."

Christopher smiled, even laughed a little.

Kari said, "Daddy, that's not nice."

And Susan wore a wry grin as if to say, "Okay, we've both said something in front of the children that we shouldn't have. Truce."

Marcus smiled warmly at her. Another disaster averted.

Christopher reached for another slice of french toast and Susan stopped him. "Not until you eat your hash browns."

"I'll have it," Marcus said.

Christopher held out the toast with a grim expression. Marcus snatched it away and plopped it on his plate in the sticky dregs of elephant snot. "Pass the apple butter, please," he said.

Christopher stuffed a sizable portion of hash browns into his mouth and chewed. He grimaced and shivered as he swallowed. "Ack."

"That wasn't so bad, was it?" Marcus asked.

"Yes. It's gross."

Marcus chuckled.

"Well, thank you for eating it, nonetheless," Susan said, forking a slice of french toast onto Christopher's plate. "And I really do want you to tell me about Bishop Penrod's lesson yesterday. You boys all looked so glum when you came to sharing time."

"Mom, I told you what the lesson was about."

"Hey," Marcus said. "There's no need to be so snotty. Your mother's just asking a question." And now Marcus found his own curiosity piqued. "What was the lesson about? I'd like to know too."

"Well, Christopher's right," Susan said. "He did tell me, or rather, I already knew what the lesson was about, but he never told me what *happened* during the lesson that made him and Chandler cry."

"You cried?" Kari practically yelled. "How—how come?"

"I—, I don't know." Christopher slumped down in his chair and glanced at Marcus, then quickly looked away, staring at his plate.

Marcus knew that Christopher was embarrassed, admitting to his dad that he'd cried during a Primary lesson. "Must have been a powerful lesson," Marcus said. "What was it about?"

"Jesus in Gethsemane," Susan said.

"Wow." Marcus nodded his head. "Yes, sir, that's a heavy subject. I imagine there's something about that that could make just about anybody cry."

"Even you, Daddy?" Kari asked.

"You bet even me. I've cried in Sunday School lessons before. And Sacrament meeting talks. Sometimes even your dad can feel the Spirit."

The last comment was meant to be a good-natured jest with Susan, but Marcus saw immediately that it hadn't been received that way. The light from her eyes had dimmed a bit. And her lips had tightened over her teeth.

Immediately, Marcus felt like exploding. Why! he wanted to shout, Why must you take everything so seriously and so personally? Why must *you* get offended by a joke at *my* expense, when you know full well that I only said what you were thinking anyway? You were supposed to smile at the mild joke and feel just a little bit guilty about the fact that you perpetually make it ever so plain that you think my spirituality is lacking.

This is what Marcus *wanted* to say but didn't dare.

Not since Susan had confessed, just the day before, through a veil of tears exactly why she harped on his spirituality. And especially not at Monday breakfast with the kids sitting right there listening to every word.

❧

Kari hated Monday Morning Breakfast.

Well, she didn't actually *hate* it, she just didn't like it very much when Mommy tried to make them all talk about churchy things. But she was happy to listen to *this* conversation as long as nobody asked her about *her* Primary lesson.

Kari wasn't ready to let anybody know that she had decided not to get baptized.

If she had actually decided that. She wasn't sure yet.

She wanted to talk to Christopher some more before she really made a decision. But now she was a little worried that Christopher might not be the person to talk to after all if he was really spiritual. If he cried at Sunday School lessons he would for sure try to tell her that she should get baptized.

"That's right, kids," Mommy said. "Sometimes even your dad listens to the Spirit. But usually, only when the Spirit agrees with your dad."

Mommy laughed like it was a joke except that, for a second, Daddy looked like he was going to be really mad, but then he smiled and said, "Yep. No point in listening to somebody if they're not going to tell me what I want to hear."

This didn't make any sense to Kari. She looked at Christopher and said, "Why-why did you cry, Christopher?"

Christopher rolled his eyes and said, "I said, I don't know. Leave me alone."

"Come on, Christopher," Daddy said. "You don't need to be rude. Besides, I want to know too. What happened during your lesson that upset you boys?"

"We—, we weren't—, we weren't upset. We were just—, I don't know. Just, just sort of … sad, I guess."

"Sad about what?" Mommy asked.

"I don't—."

Kari thought Christopher was going to be rude to Mommy too, and maybe he was, but he changed his mind or something.

He stopped and just sat still for a minute. Kari thought he might cry again.

"We were sad about Jesus," Christopher said.

"Wh-wh-wh-why?"

Christopher looked right at Kari, and he wasn't mad or anything. He said, "Because he bled so much."

"How-how-how much did he bleed?"

"A lot. It got all over his clothes, and in his hair and everything."

"What are you talking about?" Mommy said.

"When Jesus was praying in the garden he bled from every pore."

"Yes?" Daddy said.

"What's a pore?" Kari asked.

Mommy put her hand out toward Kari without even looking at her, like she was going to put it over Kari's mouth, but not quite. Still, Kari figured out real fast that she was supposed to be quiet now.

"Whatever put that kind of thing in your mind, Christopher?" Mommy looked really concerned. "Well?"

"Brother Penrod," he answered quickly.

Kari looked at Daddy to see if he was upset like Mommy. He had his elbows on the table and his hands folded in front of his face. He wasn't smiling or frowning. He just tapped his chin with his hands and sometimes pinched and pulled the whiskers of his beard with his thumbs. When he noticed Kari looking at him he winked.

"What did Bishop Penrod say?" Mommy asked.

"Nothing," Christopher said. "He just told us that Jesus suffered and bled for us so we wouldn't have to."

"You bled," Kari said, "when Clarence shoved you into the wall."

"Kari," Mommy said. "Please."

Daddy put his hand on Kari's arm and said, "We all bleed, sweetie, if we get cut or scraped. You know that. I've put Band-aids on you myself."

"Uh-huh." Duh, she thought. Why didn't I think of that?

"But when Jesus was in the garden," Daddy said, "he bled a different way."

"How?"

"Through his pores." Daddy leaned his face way down close to Kari and said, "Do you see these little tiny holes on top of my nose?"

Kari looked real close and said, "Uh-huh."

"Those are pores. That's what our sweat comes out of."

"Eeuuoo."

"We have them all over our body, and when Jesus was in the garden he suffered for our sins, and the suffering was so great, it hurt so much, that he bled out of every pore of his body." Daddy looked up at Mommy and said, "I imagine it was pretty messy."

"Yes, but—." Mommy didn't finish.

Christopher said, "Brother Penrod brought colored chalk yesterday and drew a picture of Jesus bleeding all over the garden."

Mommy gasped and said, "You're kidding me."

"No." Christopher didn't look at Mommy when he said it. And he didn't sound like he was talking to her either. He sounded like he wasn't talking to anyone at all. But he kept talking anyway. Just talking and staring at his plate.

"There was a tree. And a rock. A big rock with a squirrel on it. And a dove in the tree … that was crying. And Jesus was on the ground with blood in his hair, and on his face and running down his arms. And all over his clothes. And on the ground. His hands were together like a bowl. They were full of blood."

Then Christopher stopped talking.

Daddy looked surprised for a second and said, not very loud, "That must have—well, it *did* leave quite an impression. Wish I had been there."

"I'm glad I wasn't," Mommy said.

"Why?" Daddy asked.

"Marcus, please," Mommy said. "It's just gruesome. Too gruesome … for kids anyway."

"Maybe just gruesome enough."

Mommy looked at Daddy and frowned. "Well," she said. "A crying dove is over the top. You have to admit that."

Daddy shrugged.

Kari said, "Wh-what-what's ov-over the t-top?"

Nobody answered, nobody even looked at her. "I said—," she said.

Daddy said, "Nobody, sweets."

"But—,"

Then Daddy looked at Kari and said, "When we repent and get baptized we're showing to Jesus and Heavenly Father that we're thankful for what Jesus did."

Why was he talking about this?

"We're thankful to Jesus for what he did because that means we won't have to do it for ourselves."

Kari's eyes widened. "You-you-you mean," she said. "If-if-if … if I don't get baptized I'll-I'll have to bleed—, bleed in all, all of my pores?"

Daddy smiled. "Of course not," he said. "We couldn't do it for ourselves even if we wanted to. We're not strong enough."

But Kari felt sick to her stomach anyway. Maybe Daddy was wrong. Mommy seemed to think he was a lot of the time.

Now Kari wanted to cry. But not because she felt the Spirit. In fact, when she thought about it, she was really afraid of the Spirit.

## Chapter Five

# Monday Afternoon

CHRISTOPHER'S HEART POUNDED AGAINST HIS ribs.

Miss Farrell had gone to her desk at the back of the room a half-hour before the end of the school day and had told everyone to read until the bell rang. And now that was only a minute or two away and Christopher's anxiety was causing him to sweat and tremble.

Clarence would be waiting for him somewhere if Clarence's promises could be trusted, and Christopher's stomach ached in anticipation.

At recess Clarence had counted on his fingers all the things that he was going to do to Christopher after school. It had taken almost all ten fingers.

Christopher turned to look at the clock.

One minute to go.

Christopher nearly groaned. He put his head on his desk and felt a satisfying pain as the scrape on his forehead pressed against the Formica. He rolled his head to the side a little to put more direct pressure on the scab. It made him feel powerful to bear the pain and even enjoy it a little. Now he wasn't so frightened of Clarence.

Why did Clarence want to beat him up? Christopher puzzled on that intently, suddenly oblivious to the fact that that beating was only seconds away. While he tried to figure it out, everything else seemed so remote. All other worries and cares were so far away that they were lost in another world or dimension. With his cheek resting hard against the cool desk top, Christopher stared at nothing, and in a fraction of a second replayed in his brain every encounter that he had ever had with Clarence and still could not figure out why Clarence hated him so suddenly.

The bell rang and the real world came rushing into Christopher's world of silence and peace and safety. Christopher was momentarily confused by the bustle of children talking and clumsily lifting their chairs onto their desks so the custodian wouldn't have to do it when he came in later to vacuum the floors. Christopher's forgotten fear rushed in too and hit him in the gut like a hard-thrown ball. He hated himself for not thinking of a way to get out of this mess without getting hurt.

Every other kid in the class was gone before Christopher got to the door. In fact, even Miss Farrell was waiting for him. She was probably anxious to get into her car where she could get a cigarette. She never said a word as he shuffled past her and down the wooden steps of the bungalow. He stopped a few feet from turning the corner of the building. He stood with his hands dug deep into his pockets waiting for something to drag or push him around the corner because he couldn't make himself go. He heard Miss Farrell behind him taking keys from her purse, and as she brushed past he saw her put an unlit cigarette in her mouth. Then she went around the corner.

Somehow Christopher found himself following her, for some weird reason wanting to see the moment when she actually lit up.

But he missed it. Just as she brought the lighter to her face she walked behind some bushes as she passed through the bike rack area to her car parked on the street.

And down by the next row of bungalows, Christopher saw Clarence leaning against the wall where Christopher had scraped his forehead a few days before. Christopher's whole insides fell apart and he felt himself beginning to cry.

But then he prayed instead. Sort of. It was one of those desperate in-your-heart prayers that actually fill the whole body and explode from the ears and eyes and mouth.

Heavenly Father, how do I get out of this?

❧

Susan wandered around the house trying to figure out why she was so agitated and restless.

She went into the kitchen and poured herself a glass of juice. She drank it standing over the sink. She finished it in a matter of seconds, then rinsed the glass and set it on the counter to be washed later. She turned and looked out the window. Well, the juice didn't help; she still felt restless.

Susan watched a robin—a healthy, living one—glide over the ground and sweep to the top of the wall that separated her yard from the Alberts'. It took a couple quick hops on the wall then dropped to the lawn like a little cannon ball and grabbed a worm. Half-aloud Susan said, "You better find a good place to hide soon or you're gonna freeze when winter finally comes." That's what I'd like to do, she thought. The bird's head jerked to one side and the other, then, with the worm still spasming in its beak, the robin jumped into the air and disappeared over the house.

Christopher and Kari would be home soon.

Susan needed something to help her shed her gloominess.

Maybe I need some music, she thought.

She went into the living room and moved her finger over their modest collection of CDs hoping one of the titles would reach out and grab her. One quick skim offered her no impressions. She went back to the beginning and scanned more slowly. Most of the CDs reflected Marcus's tastes in music rather than Susan's, which was only fitting since Marcus was the one who felt the need to underscore his whole life.

Susan rarely listened to music when Marcus wasn't home, and when he *was* home she listened to whatever Marcus chose to listen to. Occasionally he would play something that they both liked, and once in a while he would play something strictly to please her—something that he *didn't* like but knew that she did. Most of those were punk groups that Susan had enjoyed in the years before she and Marcus had married. The years that she had spent with Mary going to dance clubs and fending off guys while she and Mary danced together like wild women. Marcus hated dancing, which was the only thing punk music was good for so he didn't appreciate those groups.

Susan held her finger on REM for a moment. Both she and Marcus agreed that REM was a great group though they could not agree which was their best album. Susan liked *Out of Time* while Marcus claimed *Automatic for the People* was almost a classic. She pulled out *The Best of A Flock of Seagulls*. Marcus didn't actually hate the group, but he would *never* choose to listen to them on his own.

For a few minutes, while she listened to the first song— "I Ran," a favorite from her dancing days—Susan's dampened spirits dried off just a bit, and she felt a little better. But it didn't last and before the second song was half over she was even more agitated and anxious than she had been.

Tears came to her eyes and Susan became disgusted with herself; she was more than a week away from beginning her period. This just didn't make any sense.

She didn't want to listen to the music but she didn't want to turn it off either. The noise kept her from hearing the screams of frustration in her head.

She strode down the hall to Marcus's office and went in. Though it wasn't much of an office really, it was like stepping into a world slightly separate from the real one. She could still hear the music playing in the living room, but it was meaningless. It made no impression on her. Light from the real sun came in through the curtainless window, but it didn't show her to the real world. No one could see her. That's how it felt anyway. She plopped herself into the big, comfortable, though somewhat ratty, chair that Marcus had bought at DI.

Tears spilled from her eyes and a clenching pain formed at the top of her throat where she fought a sob that ached to erupt.

Quite without meaning to, without any forethought, Susan prayed.

"Heavenly Father, I don't know why I feel so lousy, but I do. Something, somewhere just isn't right. I wish I knew what, but ... please help."

❧

Marcus glanced out the window of the bus as it slowed to pull over at the next stop. A young woman with an exquisite body stood waiting for the bus. She wore tight jeans and a cut-off T-shirt that left a lot of midriff flesh exposed to the cold air. A small unbuttoned leather vest offered little protection from the elements. She boarded the bus jauntily, with a big smile and a quick and easy greeting for the driver. Marcus could not take his eyes from her body.

After she had dropped her fare into the coin box she turned and reached up to get a route schedule from the little box near the ceiling of the bus. Her shirt went up and Marcus saw most of her breasts. He nearly gasped.

The young woman looked down at him and whispered,

"Oops." She made a face and sat down quickly on one of the benches that face sideways toward the aisle of the bus rather than straight ahead. After a minute or two she turned to Marcus and said, "I should be more careful, huh? I shouldn't go around flashing strangers."

"Whatever you think is best," Marcus said.

She laughed at that, nervously.

Marcus smiled at her.

It seemed clear to Marcus that she was fairly embarrassed by her little display of exhibitionism and was now trying to cover her embarrassment with glibness.

She leaned toward Marcus and said, "I keep doing things like that and you'll start having evil thoughts. Did I make you have evil thoughts?"

"Not yet," Marcus said.

She laughed again, then turned her attention to the front of the bus, watching their progress through town. Marcus watched her and began to let his imagination wander.

When he reached the moment that she was completely naked, Marcus smiled at himself and thought, How juvenile. Then it occurred to him that that was exactly right. He was allowing—encouraging—the formation of thoughts just like the ones he'd had when he was ... well, Christopher's age or older.

Marcus knew it was natural for him to have such thoughts pop into his brain from time to time, but he felt childish in entertaining them. He pictured himself sitting with Christopher in a closet with a flashlight flipping through the pages of a dirty magazine challenging each other on their opinions of the girls' anatomies. That's not being a father, he thought.

Marcus shook his head and looked down at his hands. There are so many ways that I could be a good father, yet in more ways than I care to think about I'm not. Mostly I'm just a lustful old lech.

I'm sorry, Christopher. I hope Heavenly Father's watching after you better than I am.

❧

Kari loved fall.

Well, she didn't actually love it, but it's arrival meant that Thanksgiving and Christmas weren't far away.

She walked the sidewalk between the rows of bungalows looking at the clouds in the sky and enjoying the cool air that pushed the clouds along.

Kari glanced toward the bungalow where Christopher's class was and saw Christopher walk around the corner and come to a dead stop. She looked to where Christopher was looking and saw Clarence Peterson waiting.

Clarence Peterson was something that Kari truly did hate and wished that she could feel good about it. She was sure that one of these days someone would really let Clarence have it, but she knew that it would never be Christopher. Still, Kari wanted it to happen and she wanted to be there when it did.

She watched the two boys for a few seconds and felt sorry for Christopher standing there looking so pathetic and weak.

She wished with all her might that, even though Christopher would never hurt anybody, he would do *something* that would really freak Clarence out. Just blow him away somehow.

As soon as she had that thought Christopher seemed to get an idea and an instant later started to run. He ran as fast as he could … right at Clarence. It looked like Christopher was going to ram right into Clarence like one of those demolition derby cars.

"Hey!" Clarence shouted as he jumped out of Christopher's way.

Kari laughed and thought, How cool!

As Christopher continued at full speed away from the school, Kari heard Clarence shout, "I'll get you, Arnold! I'm gonna make you bleed!"

Chapter Six

# Tuesday to Wednesday Afternoon

CHRISTOPHER BLED QUITE A LOT, ACTUALLY. From his lip.

He licked it and swallowed the blood. He wiped it with his fingers and wiped *them* on the grass. Christopher worked at keeping his lip and fingers free of the tell-tale stains of blood for fifteen minutes before continuing homeward.

He came into the house through the back door—through the kitchen—hoping to avoid his mom. He had seen her through the front window sitting on the couch working on some cross-stitch. Swiftly and silently he slipped down the hallway, past the living room, to his bedroom. If he could change out of his school clothes quickly enough and get outside before his mom saw him he could involve himself in some rough and tumble action and pretend that the wound had occurred then. But when he sat on the floor to take off his shoes a large drop of blood splashed on the white leather of his left shoe. Without thinking, Christopher wiped his arm across his lip leaving a broad, sticky streak of red on his flesh and beading on the hairs of his arm. He jumped up and ran to the bathroom.

He walked in on Kari, who was just pulling up her pants.

"Oops."

"Hey!"

"Sorry."

"Oo, wh-wh-what-what happened to your-to your mouth?"

"Nothing."

Christopher turned to go back to his room.

"It's bleeding!" Kari yelled it as though it were the grossest thing she had ever seen. Or the coolest.

Christopher put his hand on his lip and pressed hard, finally remembering a bit of the first-aid he had learned at a recent Webelos Scout activity. He shushed Kari as he passed through the utility room and back out into the hall.

"Christopher?" His mom called to him from the living room.

He froze. He felt his heart beating in his chest and in his ears and in his lip.

Behind him he heard the toilet flush and the lid drop down. Kari stepped up beside him and whispered, "Let me see."

He shook his head and motioned for her to be quiet. He tip-toed toward his room. He remembered, too late, that the floor creaked at a certain spot about ten inches out from the heater vent.

"Christopher." This time Mom's call did not come in the voice that asks, "Are you here and is there something I should know?" This time it said, Answer me.

"What?"

"Come here."

Christopher's heart fell into his stomach leaving an empty, but throbbing, black hole in his gut. He didn't move.

"Please," Mom said.

Christopher turned and whispered to Kari, "Get me a washcloth."

Kari went back into the bathroom.

"Christopher!" His mom was at the beginning of anger. If she had to call him one more time she'd be really mad because then she would have to get up from her stitching and come after him.

"Hurry!" he hissed at Kari.

Kari rushed to him with a sopping washcloth. Water slopped everywhere as he hurriedly wiped off his arm and hands and lip.

When he turned to go into the living room he ran right into his mom.

He hadn't figured it right.

"What's going on?" she said.

"Nothing," both of the children said.

Mom squatted down in front of Christopher. "Let me see your lip." She turned on the light in the utility room and turned his head so there were no shadows on his face. "How did this happen?" she asked.

Christopher could tell that she knew—or thought she knew—how it had happened, and he knew what she thought, but he didn't want to tell her that what she thought was right. He remained silent.

"Christopher, what happened?"

"I fell down."

"How?"

"I tripped."

"How?"

"I was running."

His mother frowned. And blew air out through her nose. Dad had said that that was a snort—a quiet snort—like the tractor in the book about the bird looking for its mother. When he was a kid Christopher laughed every time his dad got to that part. His dad could snort really funny.

Mom's snort wasn't funny.

She said, "Clarence did this, didn't he?"

Christopher looked down but didn't speak.

As good as a confession. He'd heard a cop say that to another cop on TV. "Watch the eyes. They tell all. If they look down, that's as good as a confession." Christopher shifted his gaze to the left, then turned his head to the right and rubbed his ear with his shoulder.

Mom sighed. "Sometimes I really hate that kid," she said.

Kari said, "No you don't, Mommy. You-you-you said the-you said, um, the Primary president can't hate any kids in the-in the ward."

"She doesn't hate *him*," Christopher said, "She just hates what he does."

But Mom said, "No, I hate him. He's a mean and obnoxious little creep and I'd like nothing more than to split *his* smarmy little lip."

Kari's eyes got big. Christopher shared a questioning look with her while Mom silently inspected his lip.

Finally she said, "I don't know. You might need stitches."

Christopher frowned.

Kari said, "Cool."

"We need to clean that up," Mom said. "Stay right here." And she went to the end of the hall and started rummaging in the medicine cabinet.

"I'm picking you up from school tomorrow."

"Oh, Mom."

"Don't 'oh, Mom' me," Mom said turning toward Christopher and Kari. "I'm picking you up." She pointed at Kari and said, "And you too."

"But—"

"No more buts, Christopher. I *will* be there. You won't talk me out of it again like you did last week when he did that to your forehead." Then she went back to rummaging through the cabinet.

Christopher could only stand there dreading just about everything.

"Wh-wh-what's marmy?" Kari whispered.

"I don't know."

❧

Susan waited for Marcus on the porch, holding the screen door open for him as he walked up the driveway.

He stopped a few feet from the porch and looked up at her. "What's wrong?" he asked.

"Come in and have a look at your son's mouth."

"What's wrong with it?" he asked, still looking up at her from the walk.

"Just come inside," she said impatiently.

Adamantly, he stood his ground. "What happened?"

Without a word she went into the house and let the screen door close. She was glad the spring mechanism on the door was broken because without any effort on her part the door slammed in Marcus's face. She'd be hanged before she would play mind games, or get into a petty power struggle with him.

Christopher looked up at her as she passed through the living room toward the kitchen. He still held the ice pack to his lip. Susan noticed that his attention did not go back to the television when Marcus followed her into the house. The little man-child was going to watch, listen, and send telepathic messages to his fellow man-thing so they could gang up on her. Tribal solidarity.

"Zuzu—"

"Marcus, don't even—"

"Susan, I'm sorry."

She faced him but didn't speak. Peripherally she noticed that Kari was still involved with the *Adventures of Batman and Robin* while Christopher's head swivelled back and forth as he followed what was going on between his parents. Susan looked at him hoping she could intimidate him enough to at least not watch. His gaze held steady on her for a moment then shifted to Marcus.

"All right?" Marcus said. "I'm sorry."

Susan looked at Marcus. He wasn't sorry. "What are you sorry for?" she asked.

"I don't know. Whatever I've done to upset you, I'm sorry for."

He looked so smug. He knew very well why she was upset. Why she had been upset for two days. He just could not bring himself to apologize for that nasty remark he'd made on Sunday. Well, she wasn't going to cut him any slack just because he had a hard time saying I'm sorry. Actually, those words came to his lips quite readily; what never seemed to come through though, was a true confession. He could never name his specific sins. His apologies were always generic. And now; well, now she was fairly certain that this was Marcus putting on a show for Christopher, teaching him how to become a good husband. Teaching him how to condescend. Well, watch a woman at work, kid.

She folded her arms and set her jaw and shook her head very slightly. A refusal of the apology. Even an eleven-year-old boy should see that.

Marcus's face reddened. He set his briefcase down on the couch and said, "Come here, Christopher. Let's have a look." He led Christopher into the utility room. And Marcus didn't even look at Susan as he passed by her.

Susan turned quickly and walked into the kitchen. She stood over the sink, leaning against the counter, staring at the few dishes soaking in the soapy water but not seeing them. She pinched her eyes shut to stop the tears. Several epithets flashed through her brain. It made her feel a little better just to think them. She took a few deep breaths then walked down the hall to the utility room.

Christopher sat on the dryer while Marcus inspected the lip.

"That's a pretty nasty split, kid," Marcus said.

Christopher nodded and shrugged, as if to say, I'm a man. I can take it.

Marcus picked up the baggie full of ice and wrapped the wash cloth around it again. He had already rinsed most of the blood out. He handed the ice-pack to Christopher and said, "Put this on there again." Marcus looked at Susan, then back to Christopher. "How did it happen?" he asked.

Christopher looked at Susan.

What was she supposed to do now? Lie for him to his father the way he had lied to her? Why could he lie to his mother but not his father? Or was she to tell the truth for him so he wouldn't have to admit to tribal weakness?

Marcus looked at Susan.

"Clarence Peterson beat him up," she said. "Again."

Marcus looked at Christopher.

Christopher looked down.

"Well," Marcus said. "That kid seems to have it in for you."

"Uh-huh." Christopher nodded, still holding the ice-pack to his lip.

"What about his lip?" Susan asked.

"What about it?" Marcus said.

"It's going to need stitches, isn't it?"

"Oh, it could probably do with a couple. But, it'll heal all right without them. He might have a lumpy little scar there, but that shouldn't be any big deal. What do you prefer, kiddo, lumpy or smooth?"

"Lump—"

"Smooth," Susan said.

The Men looked at her and Susan could see that Marcus was about to try to talk her out of it but she stomped all over that notion with a single look.

Susan was well aware that Christopher was scared to death to get stitches and that Marcus would fight this battle for him if Susan let him. But Susan and Marcus had made a deal with each other when they got married. Marcus had agreed that he would always do whatever Susan asked him to do if she would always ask in a kind and gentle manner, watching out for his fragile ego. Their bishop at the time assured them that it would contribute to peace and harmony. For the most part they had stuck to it, and, to their mutual surprise, it worked, but Susan was sure that some day Marcus would rebel. So far he hadn't. Maybe this would be the day. Of course, she thought that nearly every day.

Susan calmed herself with a deep breath and said, softly, "I would like him to get stitches, please." Then, before either of them could verbalize a protest, she said to Marcus, "You may not think a lumpy lip is a big deal, but I can tell you, if you'd had a lumpy lip when we were dating, we'd have never gotten far enough into this relationship to even be having this conversation."

Susan was pretty sure that Christopher wouldn't follow that trail the way she had laid it out, but Marcus would. There would have been no conversation about a child's split lip if there had been no child's lip. There would have been no child's lip if there had been no child. There would have been no child if there had been no sex. There would have been no sex if there had been no marriage. There would have been no marriage if there had been no late-night make-out sessions in that dingy little apartment in Provo. There would have been no late-night make-out sessions in that dingy little apartment in Provo if there had been a lumpy lip.

Christopher cast a hopeful look at his father, and Susan almost felt like recanting when she saw the terror in his eyes when Marcus said, "All right. Let's go."

Susan knew exactly how Christopher would interpret this. He would not for one minute think of this as a betrayal on his father's part. Christopher would naturally assume that Susan had cast an evil womanly spell on Marcus, turning him against Christopher. It would be all her fault.

So be it. Unlike Marcus, Susan could live with having one of her children hate her.

As the car pulled out of the driveway Susan stood in the kitchen watching through tearful eyes.

❧

Marcus lay on his back watching the shadows play on the ceiling and walls. The slight wind that rattled the blinds now and then was chilly, and as soon as Susan finished her prayers she would ask Marcus to close the window. More precisely, she would expect him to know that she wanted the window closed and would become angry if he hadn't done it by the time she was under the covers, lying on her side, turned away from him, ready to fall asleep.

Marcus turned his head and looked at Susan as she thought her private prayers. She was probably asking God to make Marcus as spiritual as her so she wouldn't have to work so hard to make sure he and the kids all made it into heaven with her. Yes, Sunday she had explained herself on that count, but Marcus wasn't so sure that he believed her explanation. Certainly his flippant remark was cruel, and hurtful, but he wasn't so sure that he wasn't right. And if he was, well then, the truth should hurt, and Marcus would let Susan hurt a little while. At least until she began to see that she was a little culpable. Besides, Marcus felt if Susan was all that bent on taking on the responsibility of ensuring the family's place in exaltation herself, why then he would let her. Of course, the impossibility of the task made her absolutely crazy from time to time, but he was hopeful that some day she would figure out that the task was impossible, not only because it *couldn't* be done, but because it *shouldn't* be done. Again, Marcus knew full well that it was cruel of him to appear so apathetic to her self-imposed dilemma, to indeed, make occasional attempts to sabotage her efforts, but pride and childish male stubbornness prevented him from doing anything at someone else's behest when he knew he should be doing it at his own. He would start praying again when she stopped wanting him to so earnestly.

Marcus almost reached out and touched the dark, shining hair on Susan's bowed head. Sometimes he really hated himself for causing so much anguish to occur there.

Marcus's eyes had adjusted fully to the little bit of light from the street lamp outside, and now he could see, dimly, everything in the room. He lowered his hand to the mattress and looked at the sway of Susan's back and the shape of her body beneath the powder blue nightgown. Marcus still desired her, even after twelve years of marriage and two children. Her body hadn't changed as much as Susan complained, or claimed. She was only about twenty pounds heavier than when they had married, if that much, and most of it was in her breasts, which had swelled with her first pregnancy and maintained their newfound voluptuousness even though she had never nursed their children. The rest of the weight was evenly distributed, and Marcus found the overall effect quite stimulating. For some reason he could never get Susan to believe that. On the rare occasions that he saw her after a shower, nude, in their bedroom, powdering and perfuming, she would criticize every supposed flaw on or about her body. Invariably Marcus became aroused and Susan would sneer at him as though he were crazy or some kind of pervert for finding her desirable. Lately, however, Marcus was beginning to believe that the constant haranguing on herself was some sort of pre-emptive rejection of his advances.

Well, it was working.

Susan finished her prayer and stood. She leaned over to move the bed covers back. Marcus saw dark, feminine shapes moving within the shadows of her nightgown. He imagined touching them. He looked into Susan's face. No doubt she saw the heat in his eyes, for she dowsed it immediately with "I'm really tired. I'm glad I changed the sheets today. This'll feel really good."

As she slipped between the sheets and pulled up the covers Marcus turned onto his side, away from her, trying to suppress the passion that made him yearn for her. His heart thumped in his chest. Blood surged throughout his body, never allowing his passion to cool. Marcus stared at the glow of the blue-green numbers on his clock-radio. He didn't deliver the obligatory "Goodnight, I love you" that signaled the end of pillow talk and meant that it was time to actually sleep. Even though he knew it wouldn't come, he still hoped for the soft and tentative touch of her fingers. Instead, he got "How did Christopher do at the emergency room?"

Marcus closed his eyes and sighed deeply. "I told you," he said. "He did just fine."

"I know, but—. What did he do? Did he cry or anything?"

"No. He just sat there."

"Yeah, but … what did they do?"

"They stitched his lip, Susan."

"I mean—. Never mind."

Susan flopped onto her side, turning away from Marcus, with a great deal of huffing and puffing and snorting.

About five minutes later Susan said, "Thank you for taking him."

"You're welcome."

After another minute or so, Susan said, "Goodnight."

"'Night."

Still, Marcus clung to the unreasonable hope that the fever of his desire would somehow creep across the bed and infect her, drawing her to him. Quite vividly he imagined her soft, warm body pressing against him, her arms encircling him, her hands caressing his back, shoulders, chest, her fingers playing in his hair. It wouldn't happen of course. Not even asleep yet, he thought, and already I'm dreaming.

After awhile Marcus got up and went into the living room. He sat staring out the window for a quarter of an hour. His simple desire had become an aching need. The only way now to settle the churning within him was to go for a walk. Marcus pulled a pair of sweats on over his pajamas, then a jacket. He slipped, unsocked, into some old hiking boots, grabbed a baseball cap and left the house.

Beside the fact that Susan was withholding from him, Marcus deeply resented that she used the pact they had made with each other to get things she wanted without often considering, or even asking Marcus about his feelings. There had been no real need to take Christopher to the hospital for stitches. Two was all it had taken. Marcus had only said what he had about the lumpy lip to give Christopher something to look forward to. Something to make him feel less embarrassed in front of his dad about getting beat up. Marcus was trying to make Christopher think of the scar he would get as a kind of badge, or medal of honor. But Susan had to throw some weight around and take that away from them. Now the kids at school would make fun of Christopher. Mothers had no business involving themselves in affairs like this when there was a father imminently capable of handling the situation with perfect understanding. Didn't Marcus back off whenever Susan claimed a higher authority in dealing with Kari's little-girl quandaries?

Eventually Marcus found himself out by the Village Inn, wishing he had grabbed a few dollars so he could go in, order some hot chocolate, and smile at the waitress. Maybe he would get a smile in return. *Some* kind of acknowledgment.

Marcus had been gone for nearly an hour by the time he got back into bed, and, apparently, Susan hadn't even been aware that he had gone.

Maybe she had though; the window was closed.

❧

Kari hated school.

No, she didn't hate school; school itself was all right.

Kari hated her teacher. She had hated all her teachers. Kindergarten, first grade, second grade, and now third grade. All of them were really mean. Well, Miss Ferguson, last year, wasn't so bad, she thought. Sometimes.

Right now Mrs. Winterburger was getting really mad at Jeffrey. While the rest of the class read at their desks, the Blue Circle sat around Mrs. Winterburger at the side of the room trying to answer the questions she asked about what they had read. Those in the Blue Circle were the best readers.

Then there were the Reds and the Yellows. Kari could read as well as the kids in the Blue Circle but she was in the Yellow Circle. Kari didn't like showing off. Especially for fat old Mrs. Winterburger.

Kari peeked over the top of her book. Even from across the room, Jeffrey looked really scared.

"Jeffrey," Mrs. Winterburger said, "how can you sit here and tell me that you read the assignment if you can't even tell me how to deliver a letter on a train?"

Jeffrey shrugged. "I dunno," he said.

"You didn't read the assignment."

"I did."

"Don't lie to me!" Mrs. Winterburger's loud, scratchy voice startled Kari even though she had known that the shouting was about to begin. She had seen the redness spreading up from Mrs. Winterburger's neck. "Why do you think you can lie to me, Jeffrey?"

Jeffrey scrunched in his seat, looking at the floor. Every child in the class had turned to watch. Mrs. Winterburger looked up and saw them all looking at her. But did she soften her voice? Did she tell everyone to get back to work, then take Jeffrey to the back of the room to have a private talk with him? No. Even Miss Ferguson would have done that. Only a few weeks into the school year and Kari was learning that Mrs. Winterburger actually seemed to *like* embarrassing her students.

"Class, Jeffrey here thinks that he can lie to Mrs. Winterburger." Mrs. Winterburger remained silent while she looked at everybody.

Kari looked at Jeffrey, who glanced up to one side, and then the other. Their eyes met. Jeffrey looked so sad and so hurt that Kari almost cried.

"I thought Jeffrey was a good student," Mrs. Winterburger said. "But any student who tries to lie to Mrs. Winterburger is *not* a good student. Even if he is smart and can read. Jeffrey, can you tell the class how to deliver a letter on a train?"

Jeffrey's eyes went blank. He looked like he was staring into another world. Kari had seen Christopher do that lots of times.

Everyone in the class was staring at Jeffrey. He didn't move. Until he took one deep, stuttery breath. He was holding in his tears. Kari could tell because she had breathed like that before. She felt tears in her own eyes. Kari looked at her desk.

"All right," Mrs. Winterburger said. "Go back to your seat, Jeffrey. Leave your book on my desk. Beginning tomorrow you will be in the Yellow Circle."

Jeffrey seemed to shrink.

Just the way Christopher had the day before when Daddy took him out the door to go to the hospital.

Jeffrey slumped into his seat next to Kari. They looked at each other and both had tears in their eyes. Jeffrey quickly looked away.

*That* was not like Christopher, who had looked up at Kari, through the window, as he walked out to the car. He did not look away to hide the tears in his eyes. Kari waved to him and he smiled. When he finally did look away from her he seemed to shrink. He looked like those guys she saw on the news all the time who were being taken to jail by the police.

When he got back from the hospital Christopher had gone right to his room and Kari had followed him. He laid down on his bed and covered his eyes with his arm. His breathing was a little shaky. Kari sat on the foot of the bed and said, "Can-can, um, can I see?"

Without even moving his arm, Christopher said, "Sure."

Kari moved up closer to his face and looked real close at his lip. The threads were bright blue. "How many?" she asked.

"Two."

"Is that al—is that all?"

"Uh-huh."

Kari sat there for awhile staring at Christopher's lip, then just looking around the room. Finally she said, "Did-did-did, did-did it hurt?"

"A little. They gave me a shot. That hurt."

"Cool."

They became silent again.

Kari looked at Christopher's face, the part she could see, and noticed his chin moving—shivering. He wanted to cry but wanted to not cry. She knew that feeling.

She shared a lot of things with Christopher. Once she'd overheard Mommy telling somebody on the phone that Christopher and Kari weren't like most brothers and sisters. Christopher and Kari got along with each other. They were friends more than they were enemies. Kari knew that was because of Christopher. She knew that she did a lot of mean things to Christopher when she got mad or something. But he never tried to get back at her. He was always—almost always—nice to her. At least, he was nice to her more than she was nice to him.

Kari put her hand on his leg. "I'm, I'm sorry," she said.

Christopher took one of those shivery, stuttery breaths and said, "Thanks."

Then Kari had gone to the kitchen and sat at the table and watched Daddy eat dinner. She and Mommy had eaten already. Daddy smiled at her and tousled her hair. They didn't say anything because Mommy was in there cleaning up. After she finally left Daddy looked up at Kari and said, "How is he?"

"Bummed," she answered.

That made Daddy smile. It always made him smile because it wasn't part of her language; it was part of his. He'd said once that he thought it was cute when she tried to talk like him.

"He'll be all right," Daddy said. "Don't worry."

Kari didn't worry about the lip. She worried about Clarence.

Kari came out of her deep thought when she heard Jeffrey sniffle. She turned and saw a tear fall onto his desk. He quickly wiped it up.

Kari had hardly been able to keep her mind on school all day. Earlier, at lunch, she had seen Clarence hassling Christopher, but Christopher got away somehow before Clarence started getting rough. But she'd heard Clarence say, "Just wait 'til after school, Chrissy."

The bell rang and everybody shoved their books into their desks. While Kari was nearly frantic to escape the classroom, next to her, Jeffrey moved as slow as a turtle. When everyone was sitting quietly with their hands folded on their desks Mrs. Winterburger said, "All right, class, you may line up now."

Everyone got into their assigned places in their two lines along two different walls and waited quietly. Kari hated this most of all, especially today. She had to find Christopher before Clarence did. Christopher's classroom was all the way at the corner of the school by the back fence where there were places that teachers didn't know about where you could get caught by bullies. Somebody was fidgeting at the back of Kari's line. She scowled at them. Finally Mrs. Winterburger said, "Good-bye, boys and girls."

Everyone said, "Good-bye, Mrs. Winterburger."

"Mark, your line may go first."

Mark's line was the other line. Kari huffed loudly. Mrs. Winterburger shot her a look. Mrs. Winterburger made the other line wait a few extra seconds for that. Children from other classrooms were running by outside, laughing and yelling to each other. As Kari watched, the crowd thinned out to a few stragglers. Kari was nearly crazy by the time Mrs. Winterburger said, "Rachel, your line may go."

Kari hit the sidewalk running.

## Chapter Seven

# Wednesday Afternoon and Evening

Christopher wasn't sure if he would be able to get away from Clarence this time.

At lunch Clarence had been alone and there had been teachers nearby. Now Clarence had a couple of his friends with him, and Mr. Jackson—who taught sixth grade in room B-32—had just walked by, and he was the last of the teachers to leave from this row of bungalows. Clarence must have known that, which was probably why he hadn't started to be mean yet.

Christopher stood with his back to the wall, all escapes blocked, wishing wishing wishing that he could melt into the ground and come up again somewhere far away from these boys, or change into a bird and fly into the bushes behind them to hop around from branch to branch in that little jungle chirping as if there was no such thing as bullies in the world. Christopher watched Mr. Jackson pass by the shrubbery, walk down the steps and through the bike-rack area to the sidewalk. Through the bushes, Christopher could sort of see Mr. Jackson get into his car and drive away.

"Well, Chrissy," Clarence said. "That's pretty blue thread you got on your lip. Where'd you get that?"

"Where'd you get the pretty thread, Chrissy?"

Christopher looked from Clarence to Gary, the boy who'd just spoken, then to Vernon, the silent one.

Even though Clarence was the one making the threats and carrying them out at every opportunity, Vernon was the one who truly frightened Christopher. The boy was tall and thin and had a shadowy face. He almost never smiled, and when he did, it made Christopher feel cold. Vernon always looked like the very next thing he was about to do was breathe fire in your face, then laugh like a demon.

Christopher was sure that Clarence's current behavior toward Christopher was just so Clarence could impress Vernon. Clarence wanted to be part of Vernon's little gang. Not the street gangs that you saw on the news; Vernon's crowd was just a small bunch of kids who roamed around, usually at night, wrecking people's things and scaring people. Christopher had even heard that one of these days they were planning to kill somebody just so they could see what a dead body looked like. A shiver went down Christopher's back.

"Well?" Clarence said. "Where'd you get that thread?"

"I got it at the hospital last night."

"What for?" Gary asked.

Clarence smiled. "Yeah," he said. "What happened?"

"I had a split lip."

Clarence's smile got bigger. "How did that happen?"

"I got shoved into the ground."

"Who did that?" Clarence said, pretending to be concerned.

"You did, Clarence."

Without really trying to, Christopher had said Clarence's name with just a little pause before it, and a slight emphasis on the first syllable, making it sound like he thought it was a really stupid name.

Clarence grabbed the front of Christopher's shirt in a tight fist and pulled him close. "What did you say, Chrissy?"

Christopher knew he couldn't beat up three guys, let alone Clarence by himself, even if he wanted to, which he didn't. Something told him that the next best defense was to show no fear. He certainly felt a lot of fear, but he did his best to hide it. Christopher looked Clarence right in the eyes and said, "I said *you* split my lip, Clarence." Again he said Clarence's name as if it were an adjective for something gross and disgusting. Which, at the moment, it was.

Clarence's face started to get pinker. He shook Christopher and said, "You want me to split it again? Or the other one? Huh?"

Christopher looked right into Clarence's eyes and said, "What do you think, *Clarence*? Do I want you to?"

Over Clarence's shoulder, Christopher saw Vernon smile. While it satisfied him a little to make one of Clarence's friends mock him, Christopher didn't want Clarence to know about it because then Clarence would really start getting mean, and

Vernon's smile was as devil-like as Christopher ever wanted to see.

Clarence said, "I think you want another split over here"—he touched the other corner of Christopher's lip—"so you can have some pretty pink stitches to go with your blue ones."

"Yeah, give him another one, Clarence."

Christopher shot a look to Gary, who backed up a step. Gary was just a little puppy following the big dogs around. He'd never do anything—good or bad—on his own.

"I'm gonna give him another one," Clarence said. "Come with me, Chrissy." And Clarence started to drag Christopher toward the bushes.

The shrubbery was tall—tall as a man—though not very dense. The afternoon sunlight shown through the small, light green leaves, making splotchy shadows on the ground and on Clarence's back, head, and arm, which was all Christopher could focus on with the leaves and small branches whipping his face. That and the smell of his own sweat—sort of sour.

As they left the blacktop Christopher heard Kari yell, "Christopher!"

His heart jumped. He didn't want her to see this. Even more, he didn't want her to get involved before the beating got started because these guys were just mean enough to beat her up too if she got in the middle of things. Vernon was anyway.

"Christopher, wha-wha-wha-what are you-what are you—what are you doing?"

Kari walked right up to the edge of the blacktop, where the bushes began, and said, "C-c-clarence, l-leave my brother alone."

"Shut up!"

"You shut up."

"Buzz off, you little puke!" Gary said as he reached out to shove Kari.

"*No!*" Christopher shouted it and everyone stopped and looked at him. "Leave her alone, Gary."

"Or what?" Clarence said.

Christopher looked at Clarence and Clarence tried to stare him down. But Christopher did not look away.

"Well?" Clarence said, looking away. "What'll happen if he pushes her? You gonna beat him up?"

"Nope. I just don't want him to do it."

Clarence sneered. "Tough," he said.

Just as Gary put his arm up again to push Kari, she swatted it out of the way and said, taking a step forward, "Y-y-your-you're-you're gonna be in major-major trouble, Clarence, i-i-if you beat him up again."

"Says who? Y-y-you? Ooh, I'm s-s-s-scared." And he laughed.

Gary laughed too.

Vernon just smiled.

Kari's eyes watered a little and her shoulders drooped, but she pulled herself out of it and said, "No. With-with-with my mom."

Christopher felt Clarence's grip on his shirt loosen a little.

Clarence turned to Kari and said, "Big deal. Why should I be afraid of your mom?"

"'C-'cause she's the Primary president."

Christopher knew that wouldn't matter to these guys. Only Clarence was a member of the church, and he never went to church.

All three of the boys laughed. Gary said, "Ooh, ooh, the president."

Kari turned red in the face. Then Christopher saw her expression change. She had thought of something—something to do, or say, that she was sure would hurt Clarence, and just before she said it, Christopher knew what it was.

He didn't have time to stop her.

"My-my-my mom really hates you, Clarence."

Still laughing, Clarence said, "Yeah, right."

"She really does."

Gary took a threatening step toward her. "Shut-up, shrimp!"

"Kari, don't."

The laughing stopped.

Because Christopher had spoken up Clarence was suddenly taking Kari seriously. The anger and hatred in his eyes changed. He didn't look so mean any more. Now Clarence just looked like he was hurting. His grip on Christopher loosened again.

Clarence looked at Christopher and said, "Did she really say that?"

Christopher looked down.

"So what?" Vernon finally spoke. "Who cares if his mom hates you?"

Clarence cared. Christopher could see that.

Kari beamed. "*And-and* she says you're a creep and she wants to come split your mommy's lip."

"I don't have a 'mommy.' She left."

Christopher detected a small amount of . . . something. He

didn't know what it was called, but it seemed clear that Clarence wished he had a mom.

Kari said, "Then-then who's that lady that lives in your house?"

"My dad's girlfriend."

Kari gasped.

Vernon laughed. "Oh no! Little miss do-right's gonna tell her president mommy that your dad's living in sin." And he punched Clarence on the arm.

By this time Clarence had let go of Christopher's shirt entirely.

Everyone looked at Clarence, waiting for him to react. Waiting for him to decide what should happen next.

Clarence looked at Christopher with most of his anger having returned. But it was a different kind of anger now. Colder.

Clarence poked Christopher in the chest, hard, and said, "Tell your mother I hate her too."

Then he walked away.

Gary followed like the puppy that he was, with chin up and chest out as if he had just won some kind of contest.

Vernon looked a little shocked. He seemed disappointed that no blood had been shed. Just before he turned away to follow Clarence and Gary his eyes narrowed and he mouthed the words, "You're dead." Then he too walked away.

Mom was waiting for them in the car in the parking lot at the front of the school.

Just before they got to the car Christopher said, "Don't say anything."

Kari didn't answer.

They got into the car and Mom said, "See? This isn't so bad is it? And nobody's going to bother you on the way home."

Christopher and Kari looked at each other.

"Thanks, Mom," Christopher said.

❧

Susan's stomach twisted as Kari told her about what had happened after school.

"Mommy, he said he hates you too."

Oh, great, Susan thought as she put her face in her hands.

"Mo-mom, mommy?"

"What?"

"Did-did you know his mommy left?"

Susan's insides churned and clutching pain rose into her throat, clenching at the back of her soft palate. "Yes, Kari. I did know."

"Then how come you said you were going to split her lip?"

"What?"

"Y-you, you said you were going to split his mommy's lip."

Susan stared at Kari, confusion swimming in her brain. "What are you talking about?" she asked.

"Yes-yesterday you said you wanted to split his mommy's little lip."

Susan laughed despairingly. "His 'smarmy' little lip, sweet girl. Not his mommy's."

"Smarmy?"

"Uh-huh."

"What's that?"

"Nothing. I shouldn't have said it. I didn't mean it." She looked Kari directly in the eyes, deeply, and said, "Christopher was right yesterday. I don't hate Clarence. I only hate what he did to your brother. I don't really want to split his smarmy little lip." But I do, she thought. I really really do. "I should never have said that."

Kari's eyes became red and moist. She hung her head.

Susan's throat closed off entirely. Without meaning to, she had begun to scold. She tried to speak, but couldn't. She put her arms around Kari, pulled her close and kissed her forehead.

Moments later, Susan said, "Kari, I'm sorry. Don't cry sweets. I'm not mad at you. Why would I be mad at you?"

"'Cause-'cause-'cause, 'cause I told Clarence you hate him."

"That was my fault, not yours. Okay?"

Kari sniffled but did not look up.

"Okay, sweets?" Susan lifted Kari's chin. "You didn't do anything wrong. If anything, you saved Christopher from another beating."

"I did?"

"Uh-huh."

"R-really?"

"*I* think so."

Kari wiped her arm across her nose and said, "Cool."

Any other time and Susan would have reprimanded Kari for wiping snot on her sleeve, but not today. Today she said, "Go into my room and get one of your dad's hankies."

Kari ran into the bedroom.

It occurred to Susan that if she could be kind and understanding this time, she should be able to be so any time. If I were a good mother maybe I would, she thought.

Kari came back holding the hankie in front of her. Susan wiped at Kari's sleeve to no real effect, then held the hankie while Kari blew her nose. Susan daubed Kari's upper lip and said, "That's my sweet girl. Now, where is your brother?"

"Out back. In-in the tree."

Susan brushed Kari's hair back from her forehead. Such a pretty daughter she had. And so emotional. Just like me, Susan thought. She sighed. "Thanks, sweetie."

Kari skipped off to her room.

Marcus was right. On Mt. Everest one second, in the Mariana Trench the next.

Susan walked down the hall into Christopher's room and looked out the window at the cherry tree. A little more than half the leaves had turned and fallen, making the lawn almost appear as a watercolor of bright yellow, muddy brown, and forest green. Christopher had draped himself over a branch just above the abandoned robin's nest. He held a leaf by the stem and used it to tease something in the nest. He rested his chin on his other hand on the branch.

Susan could barely make out a dark blue dot at the corner of his mouth. A mouth that frowned. Something small and bluish fell from the nest and drifted to the ground. Half of a dried out robin's egg. Christopher dropped the leaf and climbed higher into the tree. The limbs shook as he climbed and leaves rattled down to the lawn. Christopher settled into a position that left his face hidden from Susan's view. How symbolic, she thought. Christopher had been hiding from her since before he was born.

She remembered very clearly the day the nurse-midwife, Kathy, said, "I don't want to alarm you, but you should have felt some kind of movement by now."

Susan could do nothing but dumbly shake her head.

"It's possible," Kathy said, "that you may have mistaken it for gas."

"What?"

"I mean, what you thought was gas rumblings may very well have been your baby."

Susan shook her head. "Hm-mm. I don't think so."

Kathy was silent for a few moments. Then she said, "Let's give it a few days. If you don't feel anything by next week, then we'll do a sonogram."

"Should we do it today?"

"No need. Usually by this time a majority of women have felt some kind of movement, but there's really nothing to worry about just yet."

Yeah, right.

For six days Susan was a quivering sack of emotions. Until the night, lying next to Marcus—who slept deeply and loudly while she soaked her pillow with tears—sure that she was carrying a dead fetus, she felt butterfly wings fluttering below her heart. Instantly the tears of anguish became one loud sob of relief.

Marcus stopped snoring for a few seconds but he didn't wake up.

Then Susan thought something—something for which she would be guilt-ridden for years to come. In fact, she still felt guilty for it to this very moment. Instead of telling the child within her that she was happy to know that he was alive and well, and that she was glad to finally make his acquaintance, she upbraided him. She cried out in her mind, "What took you so long? Where have you been? Why have you treated me this way?"

From that moment on Susan's relationship with her son was strained at best. And she still could not get Marcus to understand. He kept labeling her troubles with Christopher as self-fulfilling prophecy. "Zuzu," he'd say, "just decide at the *beginning* of the day that you *will* get along. You start off believing the worst, and that's what makes the worst happen."

"Shut up, Marcus."

Of course, Susan never said that to Marcus directly. But here, in the silence and solitude of Christopher's room, it was perfectly all right for her to say it.

Susan dropped her forehead against the cold glass and sighed. The window fogged up, completely obscuring Christopher from her view. She reached up and smeared a swath through the fog and saw Christopher looking at her.

If only it were that simple, she thought.

❧

Marcus didn't much like being an adjunct professor, but what choice did he have? The next full professorial position would not open up for another four years. He had only an MS and it would probably take him that full four years to complete his PhD. In the mean time … hang in there. Marcus *did* like to teach, he just didn't like all the garbage that went along with being at the tail end of the pecking order. It was a little bit like his marriage; there were better parts and worse parts.

He liked not feeling alone in his life or lonely at home, but he hated having to worry about making somebody else happy. Why couldn't Susan be happy on her own? It bothered him a lot that he had to work so hard for someone else on something that came so easily to him.

These thoughts, and others like them, tumbled through Marcus's brain as he tried to read a book while walking home from the bus stop. As he was about to turn the page he realized that he had no idea what he'd been reading for the last page and a half. For an instant he couldn't even remember what book he was reading. He looked at the cover. It was *Howard's End* by E. M. Forster; one of his favorite books. In fact, he'd just read through one of his most cherished passages in all literature—"from the sea, yes, from the sea."

Marcus discovered that he had stopped walking in the middle of an intersection. He glanced up and noted, gratefully, that there was no traffic waiting on him. But then he saw that he was passing his street. If I were a Freudian, he thought, I would place some kind of significance on this. He turned around, walked back to the sidewalk and turned toward his house without even trying to read the book. When he was about six houses from home he noticed Kari sitting on the curb in front of their house, drawing lines through the dirt in the gutter with a twig from the birch tree in their front yard.

She didn't look up as he approached; nor did she even after he stood watching her for a few seconds.

"Hey, babe, whatchya doin'?"

"Nothin'."

Marcus set his briefcase down and sat next to Kari on the curb. The curb was so low his knees bent right up in front of his face. Lifting his feet so as not to scuff his shoes in the gutter, he crossed his legs then rested his forearms on his knees, linked his fingers in front of him and leaned over to try to get a better view of Kari's face. She scrunched her shoulders to hide herself.

"Doin' nothin', huh?" he said.

"Uh-huh."

"How come?"

Kari opened her mouth to speak, but shut it and shrugged instead.

This was probably one of those moments he should have left to Susan's capable feminine care, but Marcus decided if Susan could interfere between Marcus and Christopher, why then Marcus would just have to see how he could do in the moping-little-girl department.

"Why don't you talk to me, honey-babe?"

Kari shrugged again.

"I'm just your dad, you know. You are allowed to talk to me."

Kari showed no signs of having heard him. She continued to doodle with the stick.

"Don't you *like* to talk to your dad?"

Kari shrugged.

"Why not?"

The stick halted in its course through the sand. Shrugging again, Kari finally spoke, "I dunno."

That little phrase stabbed Marcus somewhere. Behind the eyes? The top of the throat? The gut? The heart? The pain was generally felt. He looked away. She really did not want to talk to him. More than the sting of sadness, Marcus was angry. He had asked "Why not?" hoping that she would deny his assumption. But she had confirmed it instead. Now he really did want—need—to know.

"Why, babe?"

"'Cause-'cause, 'cause—just—'cause."

"'Cause-'cause-'cause-just-'cause why?"

Kari threw down the stick and ran into the house crying.

Marcus sighed and swore at the street.

A few minutes later Susan appeared behind him and asked, "What happened?"

"'I dunno.'"

"She says you made fun of her."

Marcus turned and looked up at Susan but got a shaft of sunlight in his eyes. Susan was just a dark mass with its arms folded. Marcus shielded his eyes but in doing so couldn't see anything above Susan's chest. He stood, picked up his briefcase and started toward the house. He stopped next to Susan and said, "I'll go apologize."

"What did you say?"

"I thought I was just having fun. I guess not. I made fun of her stutter."

Susan didn't say anything but her head dipped a couple of inches and she looked at Marcus from beneath stern eyebrows as if to say, "You stupid man." But she was smiling at the same time.

Marcus said, "Yeah, I know." And he went into the house.

He found Kari on her bed crying into her pillows. Marcus sat on the side of the bed and said, "Kari, I'm sorry. I didn't mean it. I shouldn't have done that."

Kari's crying continued unabated. Marcus put his hand on her back and rubbed it, smoothing the wrinkles in her dress, straightening the hair on the back of her head. Eventually the crying stopped.

"Dad-daddy?"

"Yes?"

"Wh-why do I—, why do I stutter?"

"You don't."

"Uh-huh."

"Not really. It's not a real stutter. It's just—you—. I think your brain is so smart and so fast your mouth just doesn't know how to keep up with it, that's all. Everybody does—ev—, it happens to everybody. Even adults. One of these days your mouth will catch up." He stopped just short of saying I promise. How could I promise that? he thought. I may be telling her the truth, and I may be feeding her a bunch of crap. Or it could be a little of both.

"But-but everybody make-make-makes fun of me."

"I'm sorry. I shouldn't have done that. It was way wrong of me."

"I mean at school."

"Well, I'm sorry about that too, but there's not much you can do about that but ignore them."

"Th-th-they think—they think I'm stupid."

"But you're not, are you?"

"No."

"Okay then." He smiled at her, but she didn't look completely convinced. Marcus sighed; he didn't have time, or the inclination really, to try to convince her. "Do you forgive me?" he asked.

"Uh-huh."

"Thank you."

Marcus kissed Kari on the cheek and stood up. Kari wiped her cheek with her hand and said, "Yuck. You need to shave, daddy."

Marcus laughed and said, "Never."

Just as he passed out the door of her room Kari called to him, "D-daddy."

"What?"

"I saved Christopher from getting another split lip today."

"You did, huh?"

"Uh-huh."

"Thank you."

Marcus slipped away into the hall then into the living room. There he found Susan lying on the couch biting her nails. Marcus sat in the easy chair and watched Susan for a minute. Susan glanced at him finally and caught him staring at her. "What?" she said.

"How did Kari save Christopher from getting a split lip again?"

Susan sat up and told the story. As she finished, Marcus chewed a piece of dead skin from his lower lip and said, "I think you're right. She did save him from another beating. Could've been a bad one too." He spit the skin onto the carpet to mingle with Susan's bits of fingernails.

Then Marcus turned toward the window. He watched the nearly naked branches of the birch tree dip and bounce in the wind. Within seconds he was lost in unfocused reverie. And, for a moment, he felt like the loneliest man in the world.

"Will you go talk to Clarence's father?"

Marcus spun the chair around to look at Susan. "What?"

"Will you please go talk to Clarence's father?"

"What do you want me to say?"

"Well, what do you think?"

Marcus stood up. He started to leave the room but stopped. "Are you serious?"

"Yes."

"Why would?—that's—that's—it—." He shook his head. "No."

The blood left Susan's face. "What?"

"I mean. That's . . . not a good idea."

"Why?"

"Susan, we should let them work this out themselves. Christopher is a smart kid. He'll figure a way out of this on his own."

Susan stood. "And he'll get himself beat to death in the process."

"Nonsense."

"Marcus, it's not just black eyes, bloody noses, and scrapes on the forehead any more. This kid's getting really banged up, and it's gonna get worse—"

"Susan—"

"Unless we do something."

"We? You mean me."

Susan was silent.

"Listen, Zooz, it's all very well and good for you to decide what needs to be done as long as you don't have to do it. Why don't you go talk to Greg yourself?"

Susan looked down and picked at a hangnail.

Marcus started for their bedroom.

"Please, Marcus."

He stopped.

"And apologize for me?"

Marcus heard the tears creeping into her tone. He turned. There they were, balanced on the rim of her lower lids.

"I really feel—. Really bad … about what I said."

Marcus almost said, "As well you should."

The tears fell. "But I can't—. I don't think I can—. I couldn't—, myself."

"All right."

And without another word or glance in her direction, Marcus left Susan standing in the middle of the room and walked out the door.

Marcus fumed as he marched down the sidewalk. He hated this type of insidious manipulation. Yet, at the same time, he knew his anger was selfish. Marcus was the one who had been telling the elder's quorum each week that Christ's gospel was about submission. Being the quorum's advisor was the one thing Marcus felt Susan respected him for. Maybe, it suddenly occurred to him, he could get a deeper respect from her by actually practicing at home what he preached at church. Absolute submission. Even to your enemies. Well, Susan wasn't the enemy; not really. And maybe he was being a little petty. He had to admit to himself that there were times— probably more than he was aware of—when Susan sincerely acted as though she thought that Marcus was the smartest, kindest, most wonderful man alive. But even if she thought that seventy-five per cent of the time, he thought, it wouldn't be enough for me. I want people to look up to me all of the time.

As the anger began to fade, Marcus looked up and noticed that he had already passed Greg's house and was almost to the end of the street. His body was taking him to the bus stop. He turned but didn't walk. He looked at Greg's house, across the street, two doors down, wondering exactly what his approach should be. He hadn't given himself enough time to think about it.

"How do I do this?" he asked himself, aloud. Or maybe it was actually a prayer. If he stood there waiting for an idea to come to him he would never get off the sidewalk. He forced himself to move, hoping that his middling-quick intelligence might shift into high gear very soon. However, the only thought that looped through his mind over and over again as he trudged to the door was, This would be so much easier if I weren't his home teacher.

Greg answered the door holding a paperback book in his hand.

Marcus's stomach fell. This reading business also made talking with Greg difficult. If Greg would just act the heathen a bit—smoking or drinking would be good—then Marcus could take refuge in a higher moral position. The fact that Greg was "living in sin" with Janine didn't quite do it for Marcus because, even though they weren't officially married, there were some things about their relationship that Marcus envied. Greg and Janine had an easiness—a kind of comfortableness—with each other that permeated whatever room they happened to be in together. It was a quality that Marcus admired and coveted for his own marriage. Indeed, it was something that he was beginning to feel should have been an exclusive right of eternal marriage.

Seeing the book in Greg's hand reminded Marcus that he couldn't even condescend from a position of superior intellectualism. Marcus prided himself for his mind, which he thought was more eclectically well-fed than the minds of most of his fellow saints. If it were a Harold Robbins novel in Greg's hand Marcus could look down his nose, but with Greg there was no chance of that. If anything Greg was more well-read than Marcus.

"Hello, Marcus."

"Hi, Greg. What are you reading there?"

"Something you recommended. *A Prayer for Owen Meany*."

"Ah, yes. It's a very good book."

"I'm liking it."

The two of them stood on either side of the threshold nodding their heads abstractly.

"What's up, Marcus?"

"Uh, can—, can I come in and talk to you for a minute?"

Greg looked down for half-a-second and cleared his throat. Body language for "I'd really rather you didn't," but he opened the door wider and said, "Sure."

"Thanks."

As he passed the hallway that led to the back rooms, Marcus heard Clarence playing some violent video game in his room. There was the decadence Marcus was looking for. That stuff would never come into his home. Freecell was bad enough.

Greg led Marcus into the family room. Janine sat in the big chair in the corner reading *Glamour Magazine.* More decadence. Janine took off her glasses as Marcus sat on the couch. She offered him a tight-lipped smile in response to his nod. Already the ambience was grim. Greg stood next to Janine's chair. They looked at Marcus and waited. The shadows on their faces were not cast by the light coming through the sliding doors but appeared to have been carved from the inside by some perplexities of thought.

Marcus looked from Greg to Janine. Evidently, earlier, she had been working out or jogging or something; she still wore a tight-fitting Lycra suit with lots of colors splashed about and black leggings. Marcus tried not to look at her body too closely.

"Uh, well, I guess Clarence has told you about what happened after school today."

Greg nodded.

Janine said, "Some."

Marcus avoided their eyes for a moment, which held steadily upon him. "I came over, first of all, to apologize. Susan feels terrible about what she said—"

"Yeah, I should—"

"Marcus," Janine said, interrupting Greg with her delicate fingers resting on his arm, "she knows I'm not Clarence's mother. Why would she say what she did? I mean, besides being disturbing, it's quite surprising."

"Well," Marcus said, trying to laugh a little, for this was going to sound ludicrous. "She didn't say she wanted to split his mommy's lip. Uh … wh-what she said was, um, she wanted to split his … smarmy … little lip."

"Even more surprising."

Greg tossed *Owen Meany* onto the coffee table. "I don't believe this," he said and strode across the room to the bookshelves and turned suddenly. "Why didn't Susan come over here herself?"

"Well, she's …." Good question, Greg. "She's a very nervous kind of person, Greg. You know that. I guess she's afraid—she *is* afraid to confront people. Besides, we need to talk about our sons."

"What's to talk about? Seems to me Susan is the one who needs a good talking to—"

"Greg, hon—." Janine stood.

"Some Primary president she is," Greg snarled, not quite under his breath.

Normally Marcus would have bristled at a comment like that, might even have made some equally snide remark in return to defend his wife's honor, to champion her cause. But in this case Marcus felt emasculated. While Susan was normally a very fine—often inspired—Primary president, Greg's only evidence of her effectiveness was the comment she'd made about his son. From that myopic position, Susan was indeed a lousy Primary president.

Marcus watched Janine's body as she crossed the room to be at Greg's side. Marcus stood and realized too late that it was an aggressive gesture. "Greg," he said, "you've got to understand, Susan was very upset, and with good reason, I think."

Greg didn't react; other than to face Marcus with an intense gaze. Janine stood between them, facing Greg, with her hand on his chest. Of course, the idea that the two men would come to blows was absurd, but ritual chest-puffing was almost certainly imminent.

Marcus took a step backward and said, "Christopher really took a beating, Greg. Two stitches. Lotsa blood. Mothers get upset about that kind of thing."

Greg's intensity waned a bit. "Yeah, I can understand that. But Clarence didn't do it."

"What?"

Janine turned to Marcus. "We asked him about that," she said.

"I know," Greg said, "that they've had scuffles in the past, but he tells us that this split lip thing was another kid. Virgil—"

"Vernon," Janine said.

"Yeah. Vernon something."

Now Marcus stood motionless with an intense expression but silent. Marcus knew that Clarence had lied to them. His bosom fairly burned with the knowledge of it. Christopher had told Marcus on the way to the hospital that Clarence had split his lip, and Christopher just didn't lie. Not outright anyway. Sometimes Christopher had a knack for telling just the bits of a truth that could lead one to believe anything but the actual truth. Marcus himself had a talent for that. Christopher was a fundamentally honest kid despite any pernicious quirks he'd inherited from his father. And Christopher had forthrightly stated that Clarence had split his lip. Marcus could not understand how Greg and Janine could fail to see through Clarence's lie.

Marcus remembered how shocked he'd been the first time Christopher had lied to him so many years before. It was the easiest thing in the world to see through. The same with Kari. Children could not lie convincingly. Unless they had been taught. Greg, or Janine, or both of them must be pretty good liars, Marcus thought. Suddenly Marcus felt that the relationship he had been engendering with Greg over the months might be a sham. Was it possible that Greg actually hated having Marcus come around? Why that son-of-a—. But Marcus didn't want to get further into an imbroglio with these people.

Marcus said, "All right. I'll talk to Christopher again and see if I can find out what's going on."

Janine said, "We'd appreciate that."

It was easy to see that Greg wanted to bluster some more and Marcus would have been happy to oblige if this whole thing had only been about Christopher. But Marcus couldn't excuse Susan's behavior and he didn't quite know how to defend her, short of slugging Greg and shouting, "I hate your kid too!"

Testosterone hung thick in the air. Progesterone cut a swath through it.

Marcus said, "Well, I'll go then. Sorry to have bothered you." He showed himself out.

❧

Kari loved spinach.

Well, she didn't really *love* it, but she could swallow it without gagging as long as it had salt, pepper, butter, *and* vinegar. Just a couple drops.

Kari *loved* spinach.

But this fact was lost on her parents. It didn't matter to Kari that Daddy didn't notice, but she felt it was very important for Mommy to know. It was very important for Kari to do things that would make Mommy happy. Daddy said that Mommy was one of those people who had not been taught how to be happy when she was a little girl. Now the rest of the family had to help her learn.

"Mommy."

Mommy wasn't listening.

"Mommy."

Mommy had been talking to Daddy and Kari wasn't supposed to interrupt when Mommy was talking to somebody else but Mommy had stopped for a second.

"Mommy."

Mommy was drinking her water.

Christopher cleared his throat.

"Mommy."

"What?"

Christopher shook his head a little bit and frowned.

"Mommy."

Christopher shook his head harder and frowned more and looked at Mommy.

"Mommy!"

"What? I said." Mommy was looking at Kari with the mad look in her eyes.

"Um-um … um, you know-you know—"

"What, Kari?"

"Give her a chance," Daddy said.

Mommy turned her mad look to Daddy and said, "*Me* give her a chance after what *you* did today?"

"I apologized for that."

"Big deal."

"This is unbelievable." Daddy set his fork down and bent his head over his plate for a second.

Mommy said, "What's wrong?"

Daddy didn't say anything and he didn't move, but Kari could tell that he was really mad. Or really sad.

Kari looked at Christopher. He wasn't eating. He sat slumped in his chair picking at the table cloth.

Daddy said, "'What's wrong?'" And as he tried to say something else, his face got red while his mouth opened but nothing came out.

Mommy looked kind of scared.

"What's wrong," Daddy said, "is that, apparently my opinion amounts to dirt around here. First of all, Christopher didn't really need to have these stitches put in. He could have gotten by just fine without them, which probably would have kept him from being a target all over again—"

Mommy said, "It's not like this was the first time. He's been that little creep's target for weeks now—."

Daddy held up his hand and said, loudly, "Let me finish." Daddy looked at Christopher and his face got more sad than mad.

Kari thought that Daddy wasn't going to say anything. "Daddy," she said.

But Daddy didn't seem to hear her.

"Daddy."

*Nobody* heard her. Not even Christopher was paying any attention to her now.

Kari whispered, "Christopher, Mommy said I saved—"

"Second of all," Daddy said, pointing a finger at Mommy, "you've got to quit bad-mouthing that kid. Especially where young ears can hear." Mommy looked down. "Telling the world that you hate a little kid in our own ward and then sending *me* over to apologize for you … you have no idea how humiliating that was."

"I'm sorry."

"And third of all, according to Greg and Janine, Clarence didn't do this. According to them it was some kid named Vernon."

Mommy looked at Christopher. Daddy looked at Christopher.

"Is this true?" Mommy asked.

"Of course it's not," Daddy said. "Christopher doesn't lie."

"Huh." Mommy didn't believe that.

But it was true. Kari knew that. It was just one of the things about Christopher that made Kari realize that she could never be baptized. She could never be as good as him.

"It's true," Daddy said. "He may not always tell all of the truth, but he doesn't ever give false information either."

"Same as lying," Mommy said.

Christopher had tears in his eyes. "I'm sorry, Mom," he said.

Daddy said, "Don't worry about it, sport. Just don't ever mislead us, all right?"

Christopher nodded, still crying.

Kari could hardly believe it. Christopher was in trouble somehow. Kari needed to take this chance to let them know what a good girl she was being. "Mom-mom-mommy ... mommy."

"What?"

"G-g-g-g-guess, guess, guess ... guess what?"

"What?"

"I ate—, I ate all my spinach."

"Good. Thank you."

But Mommy hadn't even looked at the plate to see.

"I liked it."

"I'm glad."

Kari smiled at her daddy, who was eating meatloaf in great big bites.

He rubbed her head and smiled back. Kari didn't like having her head rubbed. But she liked it when Daddy smiled at her. He always looked right in her eyes. It embarrassed her, but it made her feel good too.

Daddy turned to Christopher and said, "Go ahead and eat, son."

Christopher picked up his fork and played with his mashed potatoes.

For a little while nobody talked, just ate, except for Christopher, who just kept playing with the potatoes. Mommy and Daddy looked at each other a couple of times. Then Mommy said, "Maybe you ought to teach Christopher how to fight."

"Yeah, cool," Kari said. But Christopher looked at her with sad eyes.

Daddy looked at Kari for a minute, in the eyes again, but she didn't feel good this time. Then he looked at Mommy and said, "Are you serious?"

"Sure, why not?"

"That's a ridiculous idea."

"Why?"

"Because I'm not a pugilist, my dear. Even if I did know how to fight I wouldn't teach my children. That's not the right approach."

Bummer, Kari thought. It would have been really cool if she could have beat Clarence up for Christopher. Christopher was too good to fight. But Kari wasn't.

"Why is it not the right approach?" Mommy asked.

"Well, it-it-it ... it just isn't."

"Says who?"

"Says Jesus."

"Oh, please."

Daddy slammed his hand down on the table and said a bad word.

Everybody jumped and now Kari started to cry. Most of the time when Daddy was mad he didn't get loud or mean. But sometimes he did, and sometimes nobody knew it was going to happen. That's what Mommy called hitting a nerve.

Daddy pushed his chair back and stood up really fast and said another bad word. Kari tried to hide below the edge of the table.

Daddy stood at the head of the table and pointed across it to Mommy. His eyes were scary and his whole head was red. "Listen to me," he said. "I don't give a sh—"

"Don't swear again," Mommy said. Kari saw tears in *her* eyes too.

"I don't care if you think I'm a spiritual sinkhole, I know I'm not. I read the scriptures too—"

"I know that—"

"You have *no* respect for my understanding of the gospel."

Daddy's voice was getting louder. And he was walking around inside the kitchen looking like he wanted to hit something. This was already worse than the arguments they had sometimes about family night. Daddy didn't like them too much. Mommy did.

Mommy said, "Marcus, that's not—"

"I'm not a complete idiot you know."

"I know th—"

"I don't get down on my knees after every verse, but I ponder, I pray in my heart, I meditate on this stuff a lot. A lot more than you or you'd understand what I'm talking about."

Mommy stood up now. "What are we supposed to do?" she shouted. "Just let him get killed?"

Clarence kill Christopher? Kari couldn't see that happening, but Mommy sounded like she could.

Christopher had that stare of his that looked like he was seeing into another world.

"He's not going to get killed!" Daddy's hands flew around, opening and closing and shaking. His voice was getting higher. "It's just kids fighting!"

"But he doesn't have to let himself get beat up."

"'Turn the other cheek,' Susan. What does that mean?"

"It doesn't mean he has to come home with split lips or bloody noses every other day!"

If Kari could fight she could send Clarence home with a split lip or a bloody nose every other day.

Christopher had his arms crossed on the table with his head on his arms. From the way his shoulders moved Kari could tell he was crying.

"Susan, if he came home *every* day with blood all over him he'd be doing the right thing."

"You're insane."

"*I'm not insane!*" Daddy slammed his fist on the table with each word. Glasses fell, and silverware rattled, and food jumped to the floor. Daddy leaned over the table breathing hard. Kari was very glad that he was not looking at her just then. Especially in the eyes. Then, not so loud, but very strong, he said, "How dare you. You know, sometimes I ask God why you and I ever had to meet."

Kari didn't know exactly what Daddy meant, but she could tell that it was supposed to be mean. And Mommy sat in her chair for a second crying so hard she could hardly breathe.

Kari said, "Mommy? I'm, I'm, I'm sorry."

Then Mommy ran to her room and slammed the door.

Kari looked down the hall with tears in her eyes and couldn't see anything really well. Mommy's door looked far, far away. Kari looked at Daddy, and he looked big, bigger than anything, and dark and shaped wierd because of the tears in her eyes.

Daddy swore again, over and over and over, sitting in his chair, banging his head on the table each time he said the bad word.

It had been such a long time since Daddy had been like this, and Kari had sort of forgotten. But it scared her so much that she couldn't breathe either. Every breath she took made her whole body shake.

Kari ran out the back door and around to the swing set where she couldn't hear Daddy saying the bad word or Mommy crying. She sat in the swing for a long time trying not to think about everything that had happened, but she couldn't stop her brain from remembering.

After a while it started to get dark, and cold, but Kari was still too scared to go in the house. Finally Daddy came outside and called her name a couple times. She didn't answer, but he found her anyway.

"What's the matter, Kari? Did I scare you?"

Kari could only nod.

Daddy's eyes were red and puffy. He had been crying too. He said, "I'm sorry. I really am. I shouldn't get like that. It's a very bad thing to do. I don't mean to scare you, I really don't."

Kari didn't move or speak.

"Let's go in the house. Okay, sweetie?"

Kari didn't move or speak.

"Please?"

Christopher walked across the lawn toward them. "Dad?" he said.

"What?"

"Um, can—, can I have a blessing?"

## Chapter Eight

# Wednesday Night

CHRISTOPHER SAT STILL BENEATH THE WEIGHT of his father's hands.

Earlier at the table, while Mom and Dad were fighting, Christopher had decided that he needed to ask his father for a blessing. It just came to him suddenly. As if somebody had whispered it in his ear. He didn't know exactly what he wanted, or expected, from the blessing, but it seemed like a good thing to ask for. Even as Dad swore and slammed his big fist on the table, asking Dad for the blessing just seemed right.

Now Dad's hands were warm and gentle. It felt to Christopher as though he were wearing a large, heavy hat from ear to ear. But there was no pinching or tightening that caused his head to ache.

Christopher kept his arms folded and his eyes shut, waiting for his dad to speak.

Outside, at the swing set, his dad had seemed really nervous about the whole thing. When Christopher had first asked for the blessing his dad asked, "What for? To heal your lip?"

"No." That thought hadn't occurred to Christopher.

"Why, then? What kind of blessing do you want, son?"

"Um …" Christopher hadn't expected this. His dad actually seemed reluctant. Christopher had assumed that because his dad had the priesthood he would know all about this kind of thing and would just take charge. He wondered how many different kinds of blessings there were.

"What's wrong, son?"

Christopher shivered in the cool evening air. "I don't know," he said.

Kari shivered too.

Dad put his arm around her and started leading them both toward the house. He asked, "Are you worried? Are you scared of Clarence?"

Christopher shrugged. "I just—." Worried? Scared? Neither of those sounded right. "I want to feel better is all."

"I see." Dad sighed. "Well," he said. "Go into my office and wait for me. I'll be in in a few minutes."

His dad's office was really a one-car garage that had been sealed up except for the door at the end of the hall that connected the garage to the inside of the house. During the winter, when that door was opened, the rest of the house would get chilly because the office had no heating vents or insulation. Dad kept saying that one day he would put in new drywall and insulation, more outlets and whatever else he needed to make it into a real office. But in the mean time, the ugly walls and bare cement floor had been covered with "creative junk" and old carpet.

Christopher liked the office. Since he and Kari were restricted from it whenever Dad wasn't home, Christopher often contrived to spend time there while his dad worked at the computer by sitting on the old love seat pretending to read. In reality he just sat there and stared at the walls and listened to his dad's music. The walls were covered with photographs, licence plates, posters, letters, drawings, cartoons, lists, hats, maps, just all kinds of stuff. And lots of his dad's books had really neat covers, especially the science fiction ones. There were not many books in Dad's library that Christopher was not allowed to at least try to read. Sometimes, if he asked, Christopher was even allowed to get out his dad's old record albums and look at them.

His dad's hands shifted on Christopher's head and were still. They shifted again and were still again. Christopher held his breath for a moment, afraid that his breathing would drown out his father's words when they came, if they came, but still his dad had not begun to speak the blessing. Christopher opened his eyes and glanced over to the love seat where he had waited earlier for his dad for nearly a half-hour. His mother sat there now with her arms folded and her head bowed. She glanced up, though, just as Christopher looked at her. Their eyes met and Christopher looked down because she looked mad.

When his dad had finally stepped down into the office, Mom was standing right behind him. Dad asked, "Can your mother be here too?"

Christopher didn't particularly want her there—he had hoped that this would be some kind of special thing just between him and his dad—but he couldn't think of a really good reason to say no.

Christopher nodded, "Okay."

"What about Kari?" Dad asked.

"Huh?"

"Can Kari come in too?"

Nodding again, "Uh-huh."

Dad called Kari into the room, then she and Mom sat on the love seat together.

And there they still sat, Kari with her arms folded and head bowed, and Mom scowling, while they all waited for Dad to begin.

Christopher tried not to think about why his mom might be angry. In his heart he prayed for a blessing.

"Christopher Jacob Arnold," his father began. "I lay my hands upon your head, by virtue of the Melchizedek Priesthood which I hold, to give you a blessing of comfort."

Comfort. That sounded all right. To begin with.

But Dad had stopped.

Christopher heard his father breathe in deeply through his nose and exhale through his mouth, but not as a sigh.

He heard his mother clear her throat, which was followed by Dad breathing in again and letting it out as a sigh this time.

Christopher waited.

"Christopher," his dad said, and Christopher thought for a second that there would be no blessing, that his dad was going to say, "Christopher, I can't do this," or, "This is wrong, you don't need a blessing." But that's not what his dad said. What he said was, "You have asked for a blessing from our Father in Heaven and … this is pleasing to him. Our Father is always willing and anxious to help his children."

It wasn't the usual kind of talk Christopher had heard in blessings, none of that scripture language. This sounded like just the way Dad talked to him every day. Every-day language. Already Christopher was beginning to feel more comfortable. He tried not to think about his mother, though the harder he tried, the harder it was not to think about her.

"Never think, Christopher, that your Father in Heaven doesn't know or doesn't care about you. He does know, and he does care. Sometimes it's hard for us to understand that when bad things are happening to us. Just remember that it's not Heavenly Father doing those bad things to you, it's another person—another child of God—who has free agency just like you do. And it would be unfair of Heavenly Father to stop everyone from doing bad things, because then we could only choose good things and then we would never learn the difference between right and wrong."

This was all stuff that Christopher knew already; he had been learning it in Primary his whole life. But it was nice to be reminded. And maybe Dad was also talking to Kari. And Mom. Maybe Mom more than Kari. After all, Mom was the one who seemed to be the most upset about this whole thing.

"But, Christopher, just because people are free to choose to do bad things to us, that doesn't mean that … it doesn't mean that there is no help for us in these situations. There is always help. We just need to ask for it. We don't always know how the Lord is going to help us, and sometimes we don't even know when he already has, but …"

Christopher wished that he could turn around and look at his dad because it almost sounded like he was crying or something. Christopher got a strong feeling that his dad was having a hard time deciding what to say next. Or had decided already but didn't want to say it, or didn't know how.

It was a long time that Christopher sat there waiting for the blessing to continue. This time he did not look up at his mother.

Dad took several deep breaths through his nose, then started to speak again. And as he spoke, Christopher got goosebumps on his neck and arms.

"Christopher, your Father in Heaven has already helped you in your current problems, and I promise you by the power of the priesthood that our Father will sustain you through whatever trials or persecutions are further heaped upon you. You are blessed with the ability to act as your Savior would. The suffering that you endure will act as a healing balm for those you love—those who love you. As long as you trust the Lord, have faith, and are forgiving of your fellow beings, you shall know peace all the days of your life.

"In the name of Jesus Christ, amen."

Kari said, "Amen."

Christopher said, "Amen."

Finally, Mom said, "Amen."

Christopher turned to his dad and saw the tears that he had heard.

His dad kissed him on the forehead and hugged him.

Kari left the office.

As Christopher followed her up the three steps into the house he heard Mom say to Dad, "Some blessing."

But Christopher didn't feel like she meant it in a good way. And for a second it bothered him that Mom was being mean. Then something warm touched him ... in his mind. In his heart.

And the tears that had been about to form vanished. And the ache in his chest went away. And the worry in his brain disappeared.

❧

Susan wished that she had the guts to be more like Eliza R. Snow.

According to legend, Eliza was a great blessing giver even though she did not bear the priesthood. Susan thought she could have given Christopher a more specific blessing at the very least. She didn't dare entertain thoughts about it being a *better* blessing. Though she wanted to.

Susan sat on the end of the bed chewing her nails.

Marcus walked in and said, "I take it then that you didn't like the blessing I gave Christopher."

"That's not what I said."

"I know it's not what you said, but clearly it's what you meant."

It was at moments like these that Susan wished she had the same lack of compunction that Marcus had that allowed him to swear.

"Well, Brother Arnold, don't you just know everything."

Marcus's lips pressed together and he shook his head slightly as he looked at the wall. He was pretending to be patient.

"No, I don't know everything," he said. "But we've been married long enough, I think I'm allowed to make an assumption now and then." Then he looked her in the eyes and said, "What was wrong with the blessing?"

"Nothing. It was very *spiritual*."

Marcus reacted as if she had slapped him, which, she had to admit to herself, she had.

His eyes burned through her for a moment, then he said, "Never mind," and left the room.

She thought a perfectly good swear word at him and flopped back onto the bed. Immediately she calculated where Marcus sat on the sliding love/hate scale. She demoted him to thirty/seventy. But when she heard him cleaning up the kitchen mess from dinner she moved him back to forty/sixty.

Susan snorted a wry chuckle at herself. She was being unfair. More than unfair, she was being cruel. She put herself on the sliding scale and found herself careening toward the shallow end. She sighed and fought back tears. The effort caused pain to clench at the top of her throat.

Truthfully, Susan knew that it had been a very nice blessing, and actually rather spiritual. She knew that the last part of the blessing was not spoken in Marcus's usual language. So it was probably the Spirit directing him. But if that were true, why hadn't the Spirit guided him to declare a blessing of protection and safety? That's what Christopher needed.

No, it's what *I* need, Susan thought. I can't stand feeling helpless any more.

All day Susan's stomach had been in a knot of worry over Christopher's safety. A hundred times she had wanted to call the school and get Christopher on the line just so she could hear his voice. A thousand times she had wanted to leave the house and go right to the school and be with Christopher; sit with him, and walk with him—like a guardian angel. If Clarence or any other cowardly little bully approached her son, she could have sent them away fearing and trembling—and bleeding from a lip or nose.

Why was God unwilling to guarantee her son's safety? Or was she overwrought about the situation? Was she still overcompensating for her guilt?

I'm a terrible mother.

How many times had she told herself that over the years?

How many times had she told Marcus?

And how many times had he sincerely tried to convince her that she was truly a very good and loving mother?

But Susan knew better. She had been a failure from the beginning. She knew that it had been a real disappointment to Marcus that she had refused to nurse their children. And it wasn't that she had even tried and merely failed. Susan had flat-out refused to try.

She had never been able to satisfactorily explain to Marcus the reasons for her refusal. None of her little lies had been convincing enough. But Susan had always felt, continued to feel, that the truth would destroy their marriage. She knew that an honest explanation would so enrage and disgust Marcus that he would take the children from her and leave her forever.

Susan also knew that it was wrong for her to hold on to this guilt. She knew that she could obtain forgiveness from God. In fact, He had probably forgiven her years before. In her heart, Susan knew that she could end a lifetime of inner torture by walking into the kitchen and telling Marcus the truth. But her mind did not trust that inclination. She doubted Marcus's ability to understand.

How would she say it? Directly?

*Marcus, when I was thirteen I tried to nurse someone's baby while I was sitting for them.*

Susan involuntarily pressed her hand to her left breast. It had been much smaller then, only a bud, and she hadn't really thought much about her development except that it was ridiculous and a little humiliating to have to wear a training bra when there was really nothing to train. So it wasn't like nursing someone else's baby was something she had planned in idle moments and plotted ways to accomplish.

The baby had been crying and Susan held it in the crook of her left arm, jouncing and swaying it as she took a prepared bottle from the fridge and warmed it under the tap. The bottle slipped from her hand as she sat in the easy chair in the living room. When she bent to pick it up her breast pressed against the baby's face. The baby turned and began gnawing at her.

The idea to expose herself to the baby filled Susan's entire body all at once, and before she thought too deeply about it, she pulled her shirt up and plucked the bra over her breast and let the baby root on her.

At first a hot thrill radiated over her like a fine net that touched her skin, then delicately cut right through the flesh and the blood to the bones. She moaned with pleasure and briefly pictured in her mind, not a baby, but a young man teasing her nipple with his lips and tongue. Then a straight line of pain shot from her breast directly to her groin. Susan gasped and pulled the baby off.

It was more than an hour before Susan could bring herself to touch the baby again to feed it. Tears streamed down her face the entire time; the two of them—she and the baby—crying their hearts out.

And now, years later, lying on the bed where she had conceived two children, more tears came. It wasn't the pain she'd felt all those years before that shamed her. It was the intense pleasure, and the lustful thoughts that had come with it that had caused her a lifetime of humiliation. From the very beginning Susan had had to keep her indiscretion a guarded secret. If her Aunt Joyce had ever found out about it, Susan's life would have been ruined.

Susan didn't like sex with her husband and she hadn't nourished her children from her own body because she felt ill every time someone touched her breasts.

She had missed out on a wonderful opportunity to bond with Christopher when he was an infant, and now she couldn't even think of a way to protect him from a bully.

While they had all sat there in Marcus's office waiting for him to start giving the blessing, Susan had glanced up at Christopher and their eyes had met. With giant hands resting on his bowed head, looking up from beneath his worried little brow, Christopher had looked frail, pathetic, and vulnerable, and Susan's heart broke instantly. She almost started to cry. She fought the tears by trying to smile at Christopher, but he looked away and wouldn't look at her again; even after the blessing.

For some reason he hated her.

And for some reason she felt he had a right to.

Susan cried long into the night.

⟡

Marcus stood in the middle of the living room fuming.

Unconsciously his eyes scanned the room for something to throw or pound on or simply destroy.

Marcus had been like this all his life. While on his mission he had worked on controlling his temper. By the time he and Susan had married he thought his anger was pretty well contained. Then came Christopher. Marcus and Susan clashed repeatedly over child-rearing philosophies and Marcus's suppressed anger began to stir again. When Christopher hit the terrible twos at eighteen months, all the old irrational passions came raging to the surface and Marcus had been embattled with himself ever since.

Marcus wrenched his eyes shut and his fingers clenched and unclenched while he took several deep breaths.

Marcus knew that Susan probably didn't mean what she had said; more precisely, didn't mean it the *way* she had said it. More disturbing to Marcus was that he was actually in a rage about the fact that Susan wasn't providing for him the physical intimacy that he so craved. Of all his passions, sex was the most debilitating; it cast a dark, yearning shadow over all the others so that whenever any other passion gripped him he was also in the thrall of his libido. While at Greg's house earlier, Marcus could hardly keep his eyes from roving over Janine's body, in fact, did *not* keep his eyes from roving over her body. Even now, with his eyes still shut tight, Marcus envisioned Janine's naked body writhing with sexual pleasure as his hands—

Marcus opened his eyes and swore under his breath.

He had to *do* something; perform some kind of task.

Become anxiously engaged ...

This is why he pursued research for his PhD with such vigor.

Though maybe he shouldn't have chosen marriage and family psychology as a major. So much of it had to do with sex ...

Marcus found himself standing in the kitchen staring at the remains of dinner.

He went to work.

Still, thoughts about Janine plagued him.

Earlier it had taken nearly a half hour to pray her and his rage out of his brain so he could give Christopher his blessing.

Marcus knew why Susan was upset about the blessing. He had tried to say the things that he thought she wanted to hear, but couldn't. He wanted to promise Christopher that no one would bother him any more, that he wouldn't get hurt again, but his mouth would not form the words. Marcus was just as depressed about it as Susan.

Marcus finished cleaning up the kitchen. He even pulled the toaster out and wiped the counter beneath it. He turned on the light in the hood over the stove, turned off the ceiling lights, and wandered down the hall past his room where he heard Susan crying.

He found Kari in his office sitting in the chair where Christopher had sat for his blessing. Marcus stood on the threshold watching her. She hadn't yet noticed that he was there. She folded her arms and bowed her head for a moment, then she looked up, unfolded her arms and clasped her hands in her lap. She bowed her head again.

Marcus smiled.

"What are you doing, sweet girl?"

Kari's head flew up, "Huh?"

"Is someone giving you a blessing?"

"Uh, uh, huh-uh. Huh-uh." She shook her head and left the room.

As she passed him, Marcus said, "It's time for bed, Kari."

"Okay."

"I'll come down and say prayers with you in a minute."

"No."

"Okay."

She disappeared into her room.

Marcus wasn't offended. Hurt some, but not offended. Most of the time Kari preferred Susan to say prayers with her. It was rare when she asked him to join her.

Marcus found Christopher, fully clothed, asleep on top of his bed. It's been an eventful day for this kid, Marcus thought.

In fact, Christopher looked so peaceful Marcus debated with himself for a bit about whether or not he should wake him.

"Christopher."

Christopher's eyes opened.

"Get into pajamas, son."

"Okay."

Marcus started to leave the room. When he got to the doorway Christopher called to him.

Marcus turned, "Yes?"

"Thanks for the blessing."

"You're welcome. Don't forget your prayers."

"I won't."

Marcus decided not to check on Kari. Let her put herself to bed tonight.

Marcus found his room dark already and Susan in bed.

She was still crying and he thought it would be nice of him to snuggle in behind her and hold her and try to comfort her. But he knew that, with Janine swimming around in his brain, and with such proximity to Susan's body, he would become aroused and that would only offend Susan.

He took off his outer clothes and slipped into bed facing away from Susan. A web of thoughts—research, blessings, work, split lips, stuttering, fighting about fighting—tangled in his mind, and through it all, images of Janine, the girl on the bus, and Susan.

Marcus ached long into the night.

❧

Kari hated the idea of getting baptized.

That wasn't true.

But now, more than ever, she knew why she couldn't get baptized, and she knew she couldn't tell anyone because they wouldn't accept her reasoning.

Even Christopher.

The idea of washing all her sins away, Kari liked. But she knew that she wasn't a good enough person to stay clean. She knew that she would need baptizing again the very next day. Probably every day of her life, but that wasn't allowed. So she wanted to wait until she was good at not sinning before she got baptized. What good was it to get baptized so young if you couldn't stop yourself from sinning?

Somehow Christopher had done it.

And now she was mad at Christopher for being so good, and for getting beat up so that he got all the attention.

See, you stupid jerk? She yelled at herself inside her head. You're sinning again.

Kari had gone with Christopher into his room after the blessing.

She didn't say anything to him but she expected him to say something to her. She wanted him to. She wanted to know what it felt like to get a blessing. She wanted to know what it felt like to have the Holy Ghost jump into your body.

But Christopher had just gotten on his bed and lain there. And then he fell asleep without ever saying a word to her.

Daddy caught her sitting in the chair pretending to be confirmed.

She couldn't figure out what to do with her hands. Nothing felt right. She had just decided that she didn't want the Holy Ghost in her when Daddy found her.

It was a sin to not want the Holy Ghost, so she didn't want to pray with Daddy. She couldn't pray if she was sinning.

She got into her pajamas and waited for Mommy or Daddy to come put her to bed.

Nobody came.

She put the night-light in the socket and turned off the big light and waited for Mommy or Daddy to come put her to bed.

Nobody came.

She got into bed and waited for Mommy or Daddy to come kiss her good-night.

Nobody came.

Kari worried long into the night.

Chapter Nine

# Thursday Morning

CHRISTOPHER DREAMED ABOUT HIS MOTHER.
He dreamed that he sat in the topmost branches of
the cherry tree in the back yard. When he looked down, the
ground was miles away and the house was a little box. But
when he looked straight out he saw the window to his bedroom just beyond the reach of the tree's branches where his
mother gazed at him through the fog of her own chilly breath.

Christopher looked away and lost his perch and fell
through the leaves flailing his arms and legs. His mother
caught him, but she didn't seem pleased about it. Her face was
set in a grim, scowling mask.

She set him on his feet then took her face off and handed it
to Christopher. While he held her face in one hand, she took
the other and touched his finger to the featureless flesh where
her face had been. She gestured that he should trace with his
finger the face that he wanted her to have.

Christopher stared at the smooth bumps where there should have been eyes and a nose and a mouth. But nothing came into his mind. He thought and thought and thought about what he wanted his mother to be but the more thinking he did the more stupid he felt. He looked down at the mask and studied the stern expression. The lips curled down just a bit at the corners and they were pressed tightly together. Her eyes seemed more sad than mad but he couldn't be sure about that.

Then he turned the mask over and looked inside. The expression there was different from the one he'd just been looking at. Inside the mask his mother's lips curled up at the corners and the eyes still looked sad, but they looked happy and pleased at the same time. Tears stood out upon her cheeks.

Christopher examined this softer face for some time then was struck by an idea that made his chest burn. Christopher held the mask up to his mother then turned it around and put the outside of the mask against her face. Immediately the mask wrapped around her head and became her real face again. Only now the smile and the tears were on the outside.

That's what you want to be, Mom, Christopher thought. Just turn yourself inside out.

Then he dreamed about his father.

Christopher found himself back in his tree looking down upon the world so far below.

His father walked around the world, holding his arms out in front of him, palms turned downward. Christopher thought that his dad looked like a zombie or something. He noticed that his dad walked through an enormous garden with lots of people around throwing things at him. Each time his father was hit with something—a stick, a fistful of mud, a piece of fruit—his father roared like a lion and gnashed his teeth and pawed at the air, but none of it stopped the people from throwing things.

The next thing that Christopher noticed was that something was growing out of his dad's hands. Christopher couldn't tell what it was at first; little bumps in the palms that had no specific shape yet. Soon, though, it became obvious that each hand had a small foot sprouting, with a leg for each one following right after.

At this point Christopher's father stopped using his hands to protect himself and started taking hits to the head and face in order to protect the little feet and legs on his hands. Christopher could see the anger in his father's eyes and became frightened as his father began to foam around his lips. Not only did it seem to hurt Dad as the thrown objects struck him, but there also seemed to be a great deal of pain associated with the growing body in his palms. Actually, each hand had only half of a body, and his father could not fully protect the halves as they grew larger. The thrown objects left marks—bruises and welts—on the body, which was now almost fully formed. Facial features were impossible to identify because they were not whole. But Christopher could see quite easily that it was a boy's body about the same size and build of Christopher himself.

Just as it seemed that Christopher's father would not be able to withstand another blow from the thrown objects he put his hands together, much like they had been as they rested on Christopher's head, and made the body whole. Now Christopher recognized the boy as himself.

And as his father attempted to shield the dreamed Christopher from the thrown objects, the dreaming Christopher saw how futile the attempt was. For there were people throwing things from all directions, and in order to keep the dreamed Christopher whole his father had to hold his hands together and away from his body and so could only shield the one side. Christopher's father bellowed one final roar of frustration then fell to his knees.

The dreamed Christopher broke loose from his father's hands. Immediately a group of faceless youth burst from the bushes and grabbed Christopher and dragged him away. Christopher's father could not stop them. He could not reach them. He held his hands to his face and wept.

And Christopher dreamed about his sister.

She climbed high into his tree carrying a golden crown with lots of jewels on it. She placed the crown on Christopher's head then sat back on a branch and waited.

Christopher wasn't sure what he was expected to do. Finally he climbed down from the tree and stood at the beginning of a broad path. Kari had climbed down and stood directly behind Christopher. Quite suddenly she threw her arms around his waist and clasped them together over his belly. Then she started pushing him along the path.

Christopher looked down and saw that every one of her steps fell in the precise location his feet had just barely occupied. Christopher looked up at the path, wary now of dangers. He didn't want Kari to get hurt.

Christopher awoke slowly and gently as he wandered down the path. After lying still for some minutes remembering the dreams, he sat up on the edge of the bed and thought, I never knew my family, until now.

❧

Susan felt Kari's forehead and said, "It doesn't feel warm to me sweets."

Kari shrugged and said, "I still don't feel good."

Susan sat on the edge of Kari's bed for a minute. Finally she decided that she would prefer the company of her daughter over the loneliness and emptiness that would crowd her day otherwise.

"Okay," she said. "You can stay home, but you can't go outside."

"Okay."

Susan left Kari's room and went to the kitchen and watched Christopher eat his cereal. She must have zoned out for a minute because it startled her when Christopher said, "What's wrong, Mom?"

"What?"

"You look mad."

"I'm sorry. I was just thinking."

"What were you thinking?"

"Um …." What *was* I thinking? "I don't know."

Susan forced a smile so Christopher wouldn't think that she was mad. Which she wasn't. She was merely troubled by something. And she really didn't know what it was.

She stayed in her chair at the table and watched Christopher take his bowl to the sink and rinse it out. She decided to call the school and ask the principal about this Vernon kid.

Christopher startled her again with a quick kiss on her cheek. "'Bye, Mom," he said and rushed out the door seeming happier than he had in days.

Susan touched her cheek. She felt a tear slide down to meet her fingers, and a smile formed on her lips.

❧

Marcus watched two girls board the bus together. They were college-aged girls, barely, and Marcus closed his eyes to keep himself from becoming distracted from his thoughts.

With his eyes closed, and despite the nauseating movements of the bus, Marcus was able to concentrate on that which troubled his mind the most—how to get Susan into therapy. Marcus wished that it weren't impossible for therapists to treat their own spouses, but it was impossible. Absolutely impossible.

And bringing up the subject in terms of him recommending another therapist was a very delicate matter. The last time Marcus had mentioned it Susan had gone into a blue funk that had lasted several months.

But Marcus didn't want to think about Susan's problems too much because whenever he thought of her in clinical terms his reactions to her became more and more sterile and then Susan knew that she was being examined.

There must be some way out of this cycle, Marcus thought.

He thought of Christopher and the blessing that Marcus had given him and puzzled about the veracity of somehow using the priesthood to help Susan. It seemed to have given Christopher some peace of mind.

Marcus didn't often trust his own worthiness to be a vessel for the Lord, even though the last part of the blessing that he had given Christopher appeared whole like a friendly phantom in his mind. It was not of his own creation.

Or maybe he was afraid that Susan would react to any blessing he gave her the way she had reacted to Christopher's.

That would hurt too much.

Marcus leaned forward and covered his face with his hands feeling besieged on all sides. Yeah, right, he thought. Poor, poor, pitiful me.

What a laugh.

❧

Kari hated herself.

Well, maybe not completely, and not all the time. But on this day she was so disappointed with herself that she simply could not make herself get out of bed.

She lay there, feeling guilty about so many things, wishing that she could be like Christopher. Wishing that she could be good all the time and not be afraid of the Holy Ghost.

Wishing that she could talk without stuttering.

After Christopher had left for school and Daddy had left for work, Mommy came in, sat on Kari's bed, and felt her forehead.

"You don't feel hot. How's your tummy?"

Kari shrugged. "I don't-I don't-I don't kno-know. It-it doesn't ... feel r-r-real good."

Mommy started rubbing her hand over Kari's tummy very lightly, "You feel like you're gonna throw up?" she asked.

Kari shook her head.

Mommy sat still, rubbing Kari's tummy for a little while, then said, "You poor little girl. Sometimes you just feel like the whole day is wrong. It would have been better just to sleep until it was all over. Is that how you feel?"

"Uh-huh."

Mommy stood up. "Get used to it," she said, then disappeared into the kitchen to make some toast.

Kari only nibbled at the breakfast Mommy made for her, and the lunch too. And even though her tummy didn't actually hurt, it did feel heavy and sort of ... dark. And it got worse as the day went by.

Mommy didn't do much of her house work; she stayed with Kari a lot, reading to her, singing to her, holding—rocking—her. Even so, the emptiness—the sadness—grew in Kari.

It grew so much—so large—that by the time Mommy came into Kari's room to tell her that she was going to pick up Christopher from school, Kari's tummy actually did hurt worse than she could ever remember. Her whole body ached just like it had when she had gone on that long hike with her Primary class in the summer. The trail had been longer than the teacher thought, and the sun had been so hot, that most of the kids had gotten sick. The memory of it made her feel it all again, only worse this time. And just as Mommy said, "You just lie there and don't answer the phone or door or get out of bed, and I'll be right back," Kari leaned over the side of the bed and threw up. Sweat dripped off her face and her whole body shook as if she were really, really cold.

Chapter Ten

# Thursday Afternoon to Friday Morning

CHRISTOPHER WALKED HOME FROM SCHOOL alone.

He had waited a while for his mom, then finally went on without her. She would probably find him along the way.

Christopher looked at the ground as he walked, thinking. He had hardly been able to keep his mind on school all day. All he could think about was the blessing his father had given him, and one thing about it in particular; "you will have the ability to act as your Savior would." Or something like that.

Being like Jesus was something Christopher had been trying to do ever since his baptism, and only sometimes did he feel like he was succeeding. But with his dad's blessing he felt so much pressure to perform better that he had started to get anxious. He watched himself so carefully all day that he wound up really not doing much of anything.

The sidewalk ended and Christopher walked on dirt, gravel, and little tufts of grass. In the back of his mind Christopher knew that he was now passing the big vacant lot that was only about two blocks from his street. On just about any other day Christopher would dilly-dally, as his Grandpa Snyder called it, at the vacant lot. The fact was when it came to dilly-dallying, Christopher just couldn't help himself. The lot really wasn't all that vacant. There were shrubs all over the place and a few trees, a couple of them really big. There were hills and bike trails, and for about half the year, a pond. Kid Heaven, Dad called it. Christopher sort of agreed.

Today, though, his mind was somewhere else. An automatic part of his brain told him it was time to cross the street and when he looked up to check traffic, out of the corner of his eye, he saw a pack of boys come out of the Smoking Tree. The branches hung all the way to the ground and inside, around the trunk, there was enough room for a bunch of kids to hang out, hidden from view by all the leaves. Sometimes younger kids, like Christopher and his friends, could use it as a fort, but usually older kids—junior high and high school aged mostly, though even some fifth or sixth graders—hung around in there smoking cigarettes. Sometimes marijuana.

For a second, Christopher thought about running from the boys who were nearly at him now, but there was a car passing so he had to wait. Besides, that would only make them laugh at him and they'd probably catch him anyway, and then they'd be meaner to him than they currently planned, if that was their plan.

Christopher stopped walking and watched the boys approach. There were six of them; Clarence, Gary, Vernon, Vernon's older brother, Sandy, who was in the eighth grade, and two other boys in junior high whose names Christopher didn't know. Clarence was not the leader of this group. Sandy led them, and when he stopped, the others stayed behind him.

Sandy said, "Hey, Christopher."

Christopher didn't answer.

"I hear you been trying to get my brother in trouble."

Christopher shook his head. His heart pounded hard, his face was hot, and his knees felt like they would melt.

"You've been telling people that he beat you up and split your lip."

"No. I told 'em Clarence did it."

"That's not what the principal said today when he hauled Vernon into his office and yelled at him for an hour."

Christopher glanced at Clarence and Vernon and said, "I said it was Clarence. I never said it was Vernon."

"Well, you shouldn't've been saying anything."

"Yeah," Gary said.

Sandy said, "Shut up, Gary."

Everyone glanced at Gary, and Christopher tried to run across the street but one of the nameless guys grabbed him and threw him toward Sandy.

Sandy said, "Come on, Christopher, let's go teach you how to keep your mouth shut."

They dragged him past the Smoking Tree and around the big bike hill toward the dead tree. Some years before, a fire had killed the tree, and now it leaned over the dried up pond like an old ghost. Christopher could not see the street from here.

One of the nameless boys said, "Nobody's gonna save you this time, kid."

They shoved Christopher into the dirt in front of the tree. A little cloud of dust rose into his face. He stood up, coughing. Grit scratched in his eyes so he couldn't see very well, but he felt a cool wind blow his hair.

Terror and the stench of a nearby dead animal made him sick to his stomach.

He heard Sandy say, "This is what'll happen if you don't keep your mouth shut," and a fist hit him on the side of his face. He felt the inside of his cheek rip across his teeth. He swallowed blood.

Somebody said, "And this," and another fist hit him in the stomach. He fell into the dust and threw up the blood. Something, a branch maybe, hit him across the back. Then they picked him up and stood him against the tree. He rubbed dirt and tears from his eyes then squinted, trying to see who might attack next.

Nothing happened for a minute. After blinking several times, Christopher saw the boys lined up a few yards away, gathering rocks. Christopher's body shook; blood and spit drooled from his mouth; tears and dust burned his eyes.

Gary threw a rock and it glanced off Christopher's knee. Vernon threw a rock and Christopher twisted and took it in the back. The nameless boys got him on the arm and back. Sandy's rock would have struck his head except that Christopher held up his hands.

Clarence hesitated, but with prodding, finally took his turn and nearly missed. It wasn't a real attempt. Christopher almost said, "Thank you."

Sandy said, "Let him have it!" And the rocks and branches and pieces of broken glass started flying.

Christopher crouched and held his arms over his head as the pelting continued. He felt a part of himself stand to the side and ask, "Why don't you just get up and run away?" "I don't know," he answered himself. "I don't know." For some reason he couldn't make his body do anything but cower.

He glanced up once and saw Clarence hanging back, not throwing anything. Just staring. Christopher tried to say help me, but he only sobbed. He saw Clarence run away. The other boys seemed to dance around like the demons in the "Bald Mountain" part of *Fantasia* that his mom didn't like him to watch.

Sandy said, "Stand him up. Hold his arms."

The nameless boys obeyed and held Christopher against the tree. One grabbed the hair on the back of his head and pulled his face up.

Sandy, Vernon, and Gary stood back with a small pile of rocks and took turns trying to hit Christopher in the face.

One rock struck the side of his head and blood trickled into his ear. Another hit his throat. A sharp one hit his forehead and blood sprayed over his face. Another smashed into his mouth and broke a couple teeth. Then one of the nameless boys got hit in the arm so he let go of Christopher's hair. The next rock struck the top of Christopher's head. And more. Many more.

He stopped feeling them.

Just when Christopher thought he might go to sleep, he heard another sound behind the mad laughter of demons.

A man's voice was shouting obscenities. No more rocks or branches were hitting him. His arms were free and he fell into the dirt. The man's voice was loud and strong and close by. Christopher opened his eyes and saw, through a red veil, a large man grabbing a boy and throwing him against the tree.

There was silence for a moment. Then strong arms picked him up. Christopher opened his eyes again and saw Clarence's dad's face. The face was crying and swearing over and over.

Christopher said, tried to say, "Don't hurt them. They're just kids."

ᢝ

Susan called Marcus at work and told him to borrow someone's car and meet her at the hospital.

"What's wrong?" he asked. "Are you all right?"

"Well, um—, yes, it's—"

"What happened?"

"It's Christopher. He's been hurt very badly."

"How?"

"Um—." Susan's hands shook uncontrollably; even her belly began to spasm. Her head felt hot and it ached behind her eyes. "Some ... some boys beat him up. They used rocks and—." Something caught in her throat.

Marcus swore.

With her eyes shut tight, all Susan could see was Greg standing on her porch holding a broken and bloody little boy.

Marcus said, "Are *you* all right?"

"For now."

"Where's Christopher now?"

"Greg's putting him in the car."

"Greg?"

"Yes."

"Why—"

"Marcus, just hurry. Please."

Silence for a moment. Then, "I'll call Will. He'll bring me down."

"Please hurry."

"All right."

Susan hung up the phone as a dark and hopeless groan rose up from her bowels into her heart and escaped as one long, silent howl. Before she completely lost sense of herself, Susan began taking slow, deep breaths, forcing the emotions back down. Her jaw shivered and ached.

Greg came into the kitchen through the back door and looked at Susan questioningly.

Susan nodded.

Greg said, "All right. Well then, we'd better go. I'll drive. You sit in back with Christopher. Clarence has gone to get Janine. They'll bring my car down. Where are your keys?"

There was a little tole-painted wooden house with hooks on it hanging on the wall next to the back door; several bunches of keys hung from it. Susan pointed at it.

Greg picked out a bunch of keys on a chain and said, "These?"

She nodded.

Greg looked at her, and she saw a score of emotions crowd his face, most identifiably anger, guilt, and sorrow. Then he said, "We'd better hurry."

Susan nodded.

She walked down the hall to Kari's room and opened the door. Kari lay curled up on her bed, still sobbing. Even now, Kari's small, but chilling, shriek rang in Susan's ears. Susan would have preferred to spare Kari this horror, but Kari had come up behind Susan as she answered the door and had seen her brother's limp body in Greg's arms, blood soaking into Greg's clothes and dripping on the porch. What was Susan to do now? Leave Kari here alone? Call somebody to sit with her? Kari wasn't really ill; Susan knew the source of Kari's feelings. Kari was sick at heart about something, so much so that her body had reacted as if she were actually quite ill. Susan had felt that way so often that at times it seemed to her that she had never felt otherwise. Susan couldn't bear to let Kari out of her sight.

She had to come with them.

Susan picked Kari up and carried her out to the car and placed her in the front passenger seat and buckled her in. Then Susan got in the back. Greg lifted Christopher's completely flaccid body so that his head rested in Susan's lap. She had meant to bring several wash cloths to try to stop the bleeding, but there was so much; she couldn't even tell how many wounds there were. Where would she begin to stop all the bleeding? She had also meant to bring a towel to protect her clothing from his blood. But she didn't care. She just watched the stain spread over her as Greg backed the car into the street and took off for the hospital.

Finally she glanced up and saw Greg watching her through the rear-view mirror. His eyes were red and filled with tears. He looked away.

"Greg."

He looked at her again in the mirror, but he didn't say anything.

"Greg, I'm sorry about what I said. About Clarence, I mean. I didn't really mean it. I don't hate Clarence. I just—I love Christopher so much—." She couldn't look Greg in the eyes any more, nor could she look down at Christopher while she spoke of him. If she did either, her composure would break. She stared out the window. "I couldn't bear ... seeing him ... hurt. It kills me a little each time one of them gets hurt. Because I wish I could be there to stop it. But I never am."

*Then* Susan looked down at Christopher and her heart broke. And, along with it, her composure.

She pulled his ruined face against her chest and cried, "Oh, my God, my God, my baby!"

&bull;

Marcus paced in a tight circle on the sidewalk in front of the Family Sciences Building.

Will had agreed to drop everything and come right over. His office was on the other side of campus, but it shouldn't have taken him this long to arrive.

Marcus glanced at his watch. It had only been five minutes since Susan's call. It felt like five hours.

Marcus took a deep breath and shook the clouds from his head. He tried to calm the twisting knot in his gut. He shook his hands down at his sides and looked high at the dimming sky. A cold wind raced down the street, scattering leaves and chilling Marcus's bones.

Will's truck squealed around the corner then pulled a U-turn right in front of Marcus, tires bouncing over the curb. Marcus was in the cab before the truck came to a complete stop.

Without a word, Will sped off.

After a minute Marcus said, "Thanks, Will."

"No problem."

Marcus rubbed his palms over his knees. He knew that Will was driving like a madman but it didn't really register. He witnessed several close encounters, but all he truly saw was a brutalized little body.

There had been times, at the beginning of his marriage, when Marcus would become extremely worried about Susan and Christopher. Often, he would call before coming home from school or work to see if she needed him to stop at the store for anything and sometimes Susan wouldn't be home and Marcus couldn't think where she might be, so of course, his imagination conjured the most horrific images. So many times Marcus had walked into the apartment expecting to find his wife and child slaughtered by some sadistic thief or escaped lunatic. Occasionally that daymare still plagued him.

Marcus's heart raced as Will dodged through traffic.

Will pulled right up to the door at the ambulance entrance. Marcus hopped out and started to slam the cab door as he thanked Will again. He caught the door and said, "Will, have you got any oil?"

"Yeah. Right here," and he flicked his key chain hanging from the ignition.

"Can you come in with me?"

"Let me park. I'll be right in."

Two sets of glass doors flew open ahead of Marcus as he rushed inside. He stopped for a second just inside the second set of doors and looked around. Greg paced the floor a few feet away and when he turned toward Marcus, Marcus's heart stopped. Greg looked as though someone had poured a bucket of blood down his front.

"Marcus. Um …"

Marcus put out a hand and leaned against the wall. His ears started to ring; he couldn't find any air.

"Marcus—"

Marcus looked up at Greg, but couldn't focus on him, didn't want to see the blood. Past Greg, he saw Janine sitting in a chair holding Kari. Clarence slumped in a chair next to them. Janine's face was drawn and haggard; she looked about twenty years older than she normally did. She said, or possibly only mouthed the words, "I'm sorry." And it wasn't just an expression of sympathy. Janine seemed to be taking full responsibility for what had happened.

Once more Greg tried to get Marcus's attention. "Marcus," he said. "They're back here. Let's go." And Greg led him toward another set of big double doors which opened as they approached.

Susan walked through the doors. Large patches of blood stained the front of her clothes, though not as horribly as Greg's. In the instant before she saw him, Marcus saw that her face was set in a grim, stoic mask. And it vanished, like the flame of a wind-blown candle, when she saw Marcus. A twisted, agonized expression replaced it and she leaned into Marcus and wept. Marcus felt Christopher's warm, sticky blood begin to soak from her clothes, through his, to his body.

A nurse appeared just behind Susan.

"Mister Arnold?"

Marcus nodded.

"Your son is in very serious condition. Your wife was just coming out here to—"

"Can't I go back there?"

"You can, but you'll have to stand outside the examination room. There isn't much space to move around in there, and there are several people cleaning him up—trying to find out—"

Will rushed in through the glass doors and Marcus interrupted the nurse.

"We want to give him a blessing."

The nurse thought for a moment. "Um, all right. Come with me."

Marcus drew Susan back from him to look into her face. She lifted her eyes to his and he said, "I'm sorry. This is my fault. Last night, I should have—"

"No," Susan said. "It's not your fault."

"It's my fault," Greg said.

"No!" Susan shouted as best she could with her hoarse voice. "It's nobody's fault. I mean—, I mean, those boys are … responsible for their actions. But, but—." She sighed and looked at Marcus. She looked like she knew what she wanted to say but simply couldn't find the words. Fresh tears spilled from her eyes and she whispered, "I'm so sorry. I'm so, so sorry."

"Hush," Marcus whispered into her ear. He rocked her in his arms and said, "I love you."

He walked her to the row of chairs where Janine and Kari and Clarence were and helped her into a chair. He kissed the top of her head, then he and Will followed the nurse through the big double doors to where all the examination rooms were. A flurry of activity seemed to flow out of one room in particular. The nurse led them to this room, where she indicated they were to wait outside for the time being.

None of the rooms had doors, so Marcus could hear everything that went on in the room where Christopher lay bleeding, though he only got brief glimpses as people moved around. Eventually, the people thinned out and Marcus could see that someone was stitching a cut on Christopher's forehead. Tubes and wires sprouted from various machines in the room that all rooted on Christopher's body.

The first real look Marcus got of Christopher's face almost brought up Marcus's bile. One eye was swollen completely shut; an ear was half torn off; his lips were mangled, his nose was smashed, and numerous cuts and abrasions marred most of the rest of his face.

"Mister Arnold?"

Marcus turned to a young man standing beside him. Marcus wiped tears from his cheeks. "Yes."

"We're going to be sending him out for several tests as soon as we get him stitched up. Nurse McKenna says you want to, um, give him a blessing?"

"That's right."

"Well, now's your chance. Mister Carter there will have to keep working if that's all right."

"That'll be fine."

"Okay. Try to make it quick, if you can."

The young man walked away and Marcus looked at Will. Marcus said, "I'll anoint. I don't think—. I don't know if—."

Will nodded and handed Marcus the small vial of consecrated oil that he had already removed from his key chain. Marcus entered the room. Mister Carter glanced up and smiled.

Marcus said, "We're going to have to put our hands on his head. Is that all right?"

"Um, sure. Carefully."

Marcus opened the vial and reached for Christopher's head. For a moment Marcus held back. In that moment he imagined how all this could have happened to his son and his stomach twisted into a tight knot. Through water-filled eyes Marcus searched for the crown of Christopher's head then poured out the oil. He placed his hands lightly over Christopher's head and spoke the words of the anointing. Will stepped up and sealed the anointing and offered a blessing.

Marcus never heard the words of the blessing. He said his own prayer in his heart. Over and over he thought the phrase, Into thy hands, Father, I commend my son's life.

Will finished the blessing and Marcus stood back and watched Mr. Carter sew the torn flesh of Christopher's face. What more can I do? he thought.

*Nothing,* came the answer. *For now.*

I need to do something. For somebody.

*Susan.*

Susan. Yes. Susan.

A torrent of memories flooded his mind. A dizzying maelstrom of images, smells, sounds, touches, and tastes that confused and calmed him all at once.

He snatched bits and pieces from the swirling cloud and reassembled memories of events he'd not forgotten, of course, but had pushed so far into the corners that they had become dusty, cobwebbed shadows.

A glimpse of thin tendrils of hair hovering like a winter's breath on the slope of skin from Susan's neck to her shoulder; the mixed scents of spaghetti sauce and garlic bread; strains of cool jazz; the feel of her lips; the taste of her tongue—

What was it? Their third date? Their fourth?

Susan had offered to make dinner for Marcus at his place. He'd done his best to set the mood with some Bob James on the stereo and the absence of roommates in the apartment. Susan piddled and pranced about the kitchen like a nervous hen, stirring up her sanity as well as the spaghetti sauce. It was becoming clear that she had an intense personality, which set off a quiet alarm in the back of his mind, but she was also drop dead gorgeous in a genuine—not supermodel—way. And he loved the crooked smile she got every time she looked into his eyes.

Marcus moved into the kitchen and stood behind her while she stirred the sauce. She cleared her throat. From that, and the tension in her back that drew her shoulders up, he knew he was making her anxious. He reached up and took one of those tendrils of whispy hair between two fingers, gave it a light tug and set it aside. He leaned down and pressed his lips to the skin on that slope from her neck to her shoulder.

"Mmm," she hummed.

She had been about to taste the sauce, but the spoon stopped and floated in the air as long as his lips remained on her skin.

Marcus stood tall and watched her sip the sauce from the spoon. Then he took the spoon from her, set it on the counter and said, "Give me a taste."

Susan twisted around and looked up at him with that irresistible crooked smile. "Open wide," she said.

First kiss.

A gray Sunday morning, four months since the wedding, in their one-room basement apartment beneath that crazy old lady, Ida, whose cracked and wrinkled face would have shattered and fallen to the floor in a hundred thousand pieces if she ever tried to smile.

The seven-thirty alarm rattled them out of sleep. Marcus whacked the clock, returning the room to a state of dim, lazy, quietude.

After a minute of silence, Susan said, "I don't want to go to church today."

Marcus wasn't quite sure how he was supposed to respond to that. Finally, he said, "Okay."

"Does that make me a bad person?"

"Why don't you want to go?"

"I have a test on *Tom Jones* tomorrow and I'm way behind on my reading."

Marcus sang, "It's not unusual—"

"Shut-up."

Neither of them had moved since waking. They each remained flat on their backs, staring at the ceiling, somewhere above which Ida could be heard hacking and spitting.

Marcus said, "How many pages do you have to read?"

"Like, a hundred and twenty-five."

The crazy idea that had been forming in Marcus's brain came to full life. He jumped out of bed and said, "I'll race you."

"What?"

Marcus knelt before the small bookcase in the tiny front room and started scanning titles. "With your reading," he said. I'll find a book that's about that long and we'll both stay in bed and read all day." He poked his head into the bedroom, "And I'll win," he taunted with dancing eyebrows."

"Seriously?"

"Yeah. You don't think I can?"

"That's not what I—."

Susan climbed out of bed and joined Marcus at the bookcase.

"Okay," she said, accepting the challenge. "But it has to be a hard and boring book. Like *Tom Jones.*"

"I'll make it a classic," Marcus said, "but I can't guarantee it'll be boring."

"Are there any short classics?"

"There's *The Pearl* or the *Red Pony* or *Cannery Row—*"

"No Steinbeck. You like Steinbeck. What about *Heart of Darkness?*"

"Or *The Death of Ivan,* uh … whats-his-name?"

Finally, they agreed upon *The Red Badge of Courage.*

They skipped breakfast, got right back into bed and read for four hours straight. At which point Susan slammed her book shut and declared, "I'm starving. What's for lunch?"

In a flash of inspired lunacy, Marcus twisted his facial features into a hideous mask and said in a garbled voice, "I am. Gi'me a kith."

"Not with a face like that!" Susan declared.

"But dith ith my real fathe!" he whined.

"Then what was the face I married?"

Marcus relaxed his features. "This? I have to squinch up my face to make it look like this so people won't be afraid of me. Dith ith the real me!" And Marcus attacked Susan.

The lovemaking that ensued was more comedy than romance but it was a heck of a lot of fun. Lunch was spent naked. As was the afternoon of reading, with Marcus crossing the finish line twenty minutes ahead of Susan at five o'clock. Dinner in bed and the evening lovemaking were both more romance than comedy.

Despite having done nothing for most of the day but lie about, they were exhausted and fell asleep in a loose, but intimate embrace before nine o'clock.

Best. Day. Ever.

Nine months and nineteen days later …

Susan's belly still looked like Ayers Rock under a sheet, but Marcus knew better than to make that allusion again. If he knew what was good for him.

Without really meaning to, Marcus and Will had pretty much forgotten about Susan's presence in the room. Well, not forgotten of course, but waiting for the Pitocin to take effect was not a thrilling spectacle, and—baby or no baby—they had a ward Christmas program to finalize, and it had to be done that day.

Susan finally commanded their attention by announcing, "You know, we haven't settled on a name for this kid yet."

Marcus said, "I thought we'd decided on Christopher."

Susan whined, "But I really like the name Christian."

"But I really don't."

"Why?"

"I told you why. It's just not a good idea."

"Oh, please."

Marcus looked at Will, who was—by this time—hiding in the corner of the birthing room. "Will, tell her it's not a good idea."

Susan shot Will a challenging glare. He cleared his throat and glanced out the window. Marcus cleared his throat as well, pointedly, so as to remind Will of his duty.

"Yeah," Will said. "It's, uh, kind of not a good idea."

"And, why is that?" Susan demanded.

Marcus and Will looked at each other, then blurted out, together, "Mister Christian!"

"Yeah, yeah, I've heard that before. But, what is it? I don't know what that's from."

Will said, "Charles Laughton in *Mutiny On the Bounty.*"

Marcus added, "I think it's in a Looney Tunes cartoon as well."

Susan stared at them for a minute. "Who's even heard of that besides you two?"

Just as the two men started to hem and haw, a strange animalish sound burbled up from Susan's throat. Marcus and Will froze. Susan panted for half a minute then said, "Will, time for you to leave. Marcus has work to do."

The next four hours passed with a spastic inconsistency. Some moments felt brief and nearly inconsequential in span, but when he looked at his watch, Marcus was shocked to see nearly a half hour had passed. Other moments stretched out for hours and turned out to contain barely a handful of minutes. Through it all, Marcus marveled at the strength of body and spirit demonstrated. in Susan's determination and complete lack of self-pity. He watched her body tremble and sweat under the strain. He felt her heart swallow the fear and the pain as she grunted and wept and bled through the process of bringing new life into the world.

Witnessing Susan's exultant joy and palpable relief as Christopher emerged from her womb destroyed Marcus's composure. For the next thirty minutes, any attempt to speak resulted in a fountain of tears.

From that moment to the present moment, Marcus had never been able to articulate the depth of his feelings for his wife, his son, and his daughter. There was something so precious, so unworldly and sanctified about it all that he couldn't allow himself to even try giving it utterance.

And now that he faced the possibility of having the holy union that was his family ripped and torn asunder, he felt lost. Completely out of time and space with no bearing for how he should think or how he should feel.

At that moment, all Marcus knew for sure was that he wanted nothing more than to hold his wife forever.

❧

Kari loved her brother.

She loved her brother so much that it had nearly killed her to see him bleeding and broken in Brother Peterson's arms.

She loved him so much that once she'd gotten over the fright of seeing him that way, she refused to leave the hospital. Refused to be anywhere but with her mom; anywhere but as near to her brother as she could be.

She had been sitting in the waiting room, with Mommy and Daddy and Brother Terris and Clarence and his dad and Janine, for a long time while Christopher was having his head and some organs operated on. They said he was bleeding inside and they were going to stop it. But they still weren't sure how he was going to be afterwards.

After Kari had cried for a long time, Mommy had cried, and Janine had cried and even Clarence cried some. Now, though, everybody was pretty quiet. Clarence's dad had gone home and gotten clean clothes for him and Mommy and Daddy. The police had come and talked to Daddy and Clarence's dad and Clarence for a while.

Clarence had been really scared but his dad told him if he didn't give the police the names of the other boys then life at home would be worse than life in any jail. Kari even felt sorry for Clarence as she watched him talk to the police.

One of the policemen had come over to where Daddy and Mommy and Kari sat and said, "Don't worry folks, it shouldn't be too difficult to find these boys and take care of all this."

"What do you mean, 'take care of all this?'" Daddy asked.

"Well, there's not a whole lot you can do with juveniles as far as prosecution is concerned, but the parents are certainly liable to a certain extent and you should be able to press charges there. If you don't know any lawyers, I'm familiar with a couple who could help you in this situation—"

"No thank you," Daddy said. "I, uh …" He looked at Mommy, whose head was down and eyes were closed. She looked up at him and Kari thought that Mommy looked very, very, very tired. Mommy shook her head a little like she was answering a question Daddy had asked, but he never had.

Daddy looked at Brother Terris too, who was standing behind the policeman, then Daddy said, "I don't think we want to press any charges."

The policeman looked surprised and said, "I beg your pardon."

Mommy looked even more tired and Daddy had that same look that Christopher got; like he was looking into another world. Mommy took Daddy's hand in hers and Daddy leaned into Mommy and rested his head against her head. Then, instead of just tired and lost, they both looked really sad, and kind of scared. Kari leaned against Mommy on her other side. Mommy put her arm around Kari.

Brother Terris stepped from behind the policeman and said, "Marcus, what are you saying? Those boys are … are … demons. You can't let them get away with something like this."

Daddy shook his head, "No, Will. I can't go after those boys."

"Their parents then—"

"Not their parents either." Daddy looked like he wanted to say something else, but he just breathed heavy and bowed his head, shaking it.

"Marcus—"

"Will." Daddy's head came up fast and his eyes were scary looking. "Don't think for a minute that I don't want to torture those—." Then he shook his head like a dog and sort of growled. "I would like nothing more than to rip those boys into little pieces all by myself. I really enjoy the thought of it."

Mommy covered her face and sniffed like she was scared or something, but she held Daddy even tighter.

Daddy took a couple deep breaths and said, "But I don't want to be that angry. I can't hate that much, Will, and be healthy …" he put his hand on his chest, "in here," he said. "I just—, I don't want to—. I don't want to be that kind of person."

Everyone was real quiet for a minute. Then the policeman said, "I hate to say this, but … if your boy dies … those other boys *will* be held accountable."

Kari felt her stomach turn again, and heat spread over her face. If Christopher died … well, he just couldn't. He couldn't.

Daddy had finally told the policeman to do whatever was right by the law but to leave the family out of it as much as possible. Like Brother Terris said, it would be terrible if those bad boys did the same thing to someone else because they were allowed to get away with hurting Christopher. Kari wished that those boys just didn't even exist.

After all that, some ladies from the ward had come and talked to Mommy for a little bit and said they would take Kari home with them, but Kari and Mommy refused.

The bishop had come too.

But now it was the middle of the night and they were all alone again.

Daddy had not let go of Mommy very much all night. They held each other and whispered to each other and looked at each other in the eyes. Brother Peterson was more upset than Mommy or Daddy were, and Janine looked small and lonely. Clarence looked like he wanted to die. Kari felt sorry for him.

And everybody just looked sad.

Kari remembered that once she had been really sad about something—a broken doll—and Christopher had prayed with her so she wouldn't feel so sad. Mommy and Daddy had smiled when Kari told them about it and she thought they were laughing at her. She had felt stupid for praying not to be sad. But Christopher told her they had smiled because they were happy that she and Christopher had prayed together.

Kari got up from her chair and went to get a drink at the fountain. When she turned around she was shocked at how dark it was in the waiting room. Everybody just looked like shadows of rocks; not moving, bent over, staring at the floor.

Kari felt a sudden need to pray. But she didn't want to do it in front of everybody.

There was a great big fish tank that separated the part of the waiting room they all sat in from a smaller section. Kari went to that area and kneeled at one of the chairs there. But she didn't know exactly what to say; she just knew that she was really, really sad and she wanted Heavenly Father to help her not be so sad. She linked her fingers and set her hands softly on the chair and rested her forehead on her top thumb, and whispered, "D-d-d-d … dear … Heavenly … F-f-f-f-f—." and she stopped.

"Kari?"

Mommy's voice scared Kari, but she didn't jump up or anything. She didn't even turn around. She said, "What?"

Mommy came and knelt by her and said, "Can I pray with you? Your dad and I?"

Kari turned around and saw Daddy standing by the corner of the fish tank.

"Um-um-um, okay."

Daddy came and squatted by her chair and said in a soft voice, "Let's ask Greg and Janine and Clarence too, okay?"

Kari couldn't see them but she thought about how sad and lonely they looked all bent over and separate in their chairs, not really connected to each other the way Mommy and Daddy and Kari had been most of the night. She felt embarrassed about inviting them over but she nodded her head anyway.

Daddy went back to the corner of the fish tank and spoke to Brother Peterson. "Greg," he said, "we're going to have a family prayer over here. We'd really like it if you joined us. You too, Will."

Kari heard Janine say, "We don't deserve—"

Mommy stood up and called around the fish tank, "Yes you do."

Greg said, "It's very nice of you, but I'd feel … out of place, I guess."

Daddy said, "Come on, Greg. Join us."

Finally, they came into this smaller section of the waiting room and all knelt in a circle sort of. Daddy looked at Kari and said, "Will you lead us?"

"You-you-you want, you want me to say it?"

Daddy nodded.

"Out-out-out-out-out-out loud?"

"Yes."

"I—, I can't, I can't, I—"

"You can do it, sweets."

Daddy looked her in the eyes and smiled.

Kari looked at Mommy.

Mommy smiled too and nodded.

So Kari bowed her head and prayed. And she knew that even if she stuttered, Heavenly Father would listen anyway. She also knew that if she really did want to stop feeling so sad, if she asked, Heavenly Father would help her. He would help them all.

Her big brother Christopher had taught her that.

# Epilogue

CHRISTOPHER JACOB ARNOLD SLEPT PEACE-fully for many days before he woke again.

# Acknowledgments

This book is more than twenty years old, I know that much. But when I actually started the writing process, I couldn't tell you with any precision. I know it was while I was still an active member of the critique group Xenobia.

Though Xenobia was/is primarily devoted to the science fiction and fantasy genres, they let me bring in a short story called "The Whipping Boy" that was decidedly not science fiction or fantasy. They had a variety of criticisms and suggestions for improvement, the most common being that the story was too short. They all wanted it to start much earlier than it did. What is now chapter six is where the first version began. Also, they urged me to change the title because of that Newbery book that stole my title years before I wrote my book. Thanks to all those Xenobians—too many to name. (Though I will mention one by name: Bill Shunn. (Bill was one of the guys who started a sort of Xenobia splinter group,

Pilgimage—made up of a few Xenobians and a few non-Xenobians—this group burned hot for two years then ran out of fuel. It was a thrilling time, but *The Agitated Heart* was never vetted by that group.) Xenobia met every Saturday night and after each critique session, some of us went out to eat; writers love to eat and talk. After the restaurant, Bill and I would stand around in the parking lot for another hour and a half, just talking. After the fifth or sixth time I came to bed at one or two o' the clock with frigid skin, my wife said, "Bring the boy home if you want to talk." (Why hadn't we thought of that?) Bill did come home with me and for a year and a half, he hardly ever wasn't in our home. We spent hours and hours talking about … everything. He became a True Friend, not just to me but to my wife and our kids as well. He ate with us, watched TV with us, birthday partied with us, prayed with us, and played with us until he fell in love and moved away to a bigger city. All of that talking and time spent with Bill still informs the why and how of my writing: Thank you, Bill.) *The Whipping Boy* grew to be three times its original size and went through three titles before all was said and done. Good call, guys. And, thank you.

Before the Internet became a Thing, there were listserves that allowed groups of people to discuss various things through email. I got hooked up with a listserv sponsored by the Association for Mormon Letters (AML). I became friends with several of its subscribers. Some of them read my manuscript and listened to my woes about trying to get the thing published. They were supportive and encouraging. Again, there are too many to name (I, once more, will name one: Darlene Young. We met at an AML event of some kind in the Provo Library. We sat apart from the crowd, two Fringers, trying to get the lay of the land before throwing ourselves into the fray. We introduced ourselves to each other and began to chat a little. It didn't take long for us to forget there ever was a fray on land of which we needed to get the lay. She instantly became a surrogate little sister for me, a tiny and cute little girl who was smart, intelligent (more so than me, which is actually thrilling, to be truthful), who has bolstered and encouraged me along for many years. And, more importantly, has been honest and insightful with all her criticisms of my work; an invaluable friend.), but I love and thank them all.

There is one person, though, who has championed this little book from the very beginning. He was a fellow Xenobian, Pilgrim, and AMLer. Scott Parkin, through years and years of high times and low times (for both of us and our families) has stood by my little domestic drama with loyalty and conviction. He has a very keen critical and analytical mind, a mind that I admire and trust. So, when he sat with me (or were we standing in a parking lot, talking over the top of a car until the wee, frigid hours of a morning?) and told me things about this story that I was unaware of, I listened. And I learned a few things about the writing process; things that have made me a better writer.

When Scott said that he wanted to publish my book some day, I told him that I would let him. And now that both of us are nestled in the nadir of a low time, he has let me force him into following through with that threat. I can't thank him and Marny (Scott's lovely, smart, and talented wife and partner) enough for their faith in me and my troubling little tale.

Scott, maybe there is finally an audience for a book like this. Maybe they'll even buy a few copies.

Finally, this kind of thing doesn't happen without the love and support of my greatest champion, my wife, Lynne. She has loved this book from its birth. I am grateful for her fierce defense of its merits. But, Sweetie, listen, no matter what you say, you are not Susan.

J. Scott Bronson
Orem, April 2015

# About the Author

J. Scott Bronson, originally from San Diego, now lives in Utah with his wife and the single remaining child of five who has yet to move out. All through junior high, high school, and college, he studied the theatrical arts, focusing on acting, directing, and playwriting. Two of his plays are Mayhew Award winners. Another, *Stones,* won the Association for Mormon Letters' 2001 award for best drama. Stones also appears in the anthology *Saints on Stage.* Though written more than twenty years ago, *The Agitated Heart* is his first published novel. A small collection of science fiction short stories, *Darkness on the Edge of Light,* also published by ArcPoint Media, appeared in 2013.